I0819920

The Star & Cicatrix Legacy Book One

A STAR APPEARS

Addison Dixon

The characters and events in this book are fictional, and any resemblance to actual persons and events is coincidental.

Published by Starstruck

www.addisondixon.com

Cover design & interior formatting by Emilie Haney of www.eahcreative.com

Vabella Publishing published an earlier edition of this book.

For my parents.
Ya'll have always been there to encourage and support me from the day I started writing this book to follow my dreams and pursue my calling.

Before...

In the quiet of the late evening, within the world of Leíso, the village of L'Za sat against the pink and violet horizon. A faint orange glow illuminated the village and peace rested upon the People of the Symbol.

A midwife tended the fire within a little hovel as a young mother birthed her last child. She'd had two other children before—one sickly, the other stillborn. This child was her final attempt.

"He is alive!" the midwife exclaimed. "The child is alive!"

Tears trickled down the mother's cheeks. However, the moment she took the baby into her arms, she gasped—as did her husband and the midwife.

"He has a star!" The babe's father gently stroked his thumb above the child's eye. The star stood out on the outer corner of the baby's eye, as though painted with black ink. "What could this mean? Is it a mistake?"

"Shh!" the mother scolded. "Do not speak of such nonsense!"

But it was true—the child had a star . . . a mark unseen for generations.

"It must be a sign," the midwife pointed out. "The legends do state that a star is a symbol of bravery, and he is the second child to have one."

The parents wondered what this could possibly signify. In the meantime, the babe's mother held him, tenderly stroking his soft head as he suckled.

At nine years old, the child grew into his star. The People of the Symbol, however, were unaware of the danger this strong, bold child posed to their lives.

One day, as the villagers tended their gardens, visited neighbors, and worked the fields to prepare for winter, a billow of black mist filled the air at the village gate. The mist blocked out the sun, sending shivers through the village.

All activity stalled as a figure formed in the mist. A tall, armored man stepped forth. His deep blue, inhuman eyes roved over the villagers until his malicious gaze landed on Órtheod, the village leader, who was visiting the family of the boy with the star.

Órtheod reached for his sword, but he'd left it in his hovel. Keeping his distance, he demanded, "What do you want, demolic?"

The Dark Magician stared Órtheod down. His sharp eyes missed nothing. Around him, the frightened people sidled away.

With a bitter smile, the Dark Magician examined the villagers. When his gaze landed upon the child with the star, his demeanor changed, exposing unconcealed wrath. "I am here to murder and abolish," he hissed, drawing his sword. "That child is a threat I must eradicate." He pointed the long sword at the boy, who stood with his parents. "He must not grow into a man and live to defeat me!"

The parents' eyes widened in horror as the Dark Magician advanced towards their child.

"Attack the demolic!" Órtheod shouted. But the Dark Magician sent bursts of violet flames towards those who dared, cutting them down and engulfing them on the spot. Screaming, the remaining villagers tried to flee from the monster destroying their village.

Someone handed Órtheod a sword. He charged the Dark Magician, fighting the demolic until a bolt of dark lightning flew from the demolic's hand and struck and killed the village leader.

The boy's parents tried to hide their child, but the demolic shot a bolt of dark lightning straight for the little family, killing them all instantly.

Soon, all of the villagers were slain. The Dark Magician stood amidst the flames. He smiled maliciously as he looked on at the boy's body.

A flash of light appeared in his periphery. A moment later, a man with grayish-brown hair reaching close to his shoulders and piercing emerald-green eyes, ran through the village entrance, his russet cape blowing in the wind.

The man paused amidst the carnage, taking in the bodies and destruction. His mouth pulled into a frown.

"See this, you fool?" the Dark Magician smiled and gestured around. "I have done this! I have even destroyed the one with the star!"

The Light Magician followed the direction of the Dark Magician's gaze, resting on the child's body.

The Dark Magician chuckled—a strange, gurgling sound. "I will have no other threats!"

The Light Magician looked at the gloating demolic. "You do realize there will be another?"

The Dark Magician paused, and then growled, "Another what?"

The Light Magician motioned to the boy. "Another one with a star. The legends state a third child will bear the star," he said, adding, "and he *will* defeat you."

The Dark Magician's eyes flashed. "Then I will kill him, as well." His lips curled into a vicious sneer. "He will not live to defeat me."

Chapter One

Riley's eyes glazed over as he scrolled through the playlist on his phone, deleting songs. Many of them he never listened to, so why keep them? Every once in a while, he bit into his turkey and cheese sandwich while sitting in a tree behind his high school cafeteria. He was not into lunchroom drama. Besides, the tree offered pleasant shade on warm days.

"For the last time, no. I'm not interested."

Riley carefully scooted up on the branch and peeked through the leaves. Yep. It was her. His friend Caroline with whom he'd been friends since fourth grade. Her long brown hair fell across a lavender t-shirt. Caroline stood in front of the tree Riley perched in but didn't seem to notice him. She lifted her arm as though warding off something unpleasant.

"Why not?" A male voice. Riley craned his neck a little and spotted a dark-haired guy wearing a red shirt. What was he doing?

"I have no interest in anyone. I don't want to go on a date." Caroline took a step back.

The guy, clearly not listening, came closer. "Are you going out with anyone else?"

"What's it matter to you?" Caroline retorted.

What was this guy's problem? Why couldn't he take no for an answer?

"I just want to know. I haven't seen you with anyone else."

"Because I'm *not* with anyone else! Now leave me alone!" Caroline turned to go. To Riley's shock, the guy reached out and touched Caroline's hair. Caroline spun on the guy in disgust.

Riley stuffed his phone into his pocket and his sandwich into a bag, then grabbed a branch to his right—hanging close to the ground—and swung down. He was angry enough to kick his heels into the guy's chest to push him back but didn't want to cause a scene. Even though Riley of average height, this guy was almost a head taller than him. Riley's stomach dropped. "Dude, she said *leave her alone.*" Riley stood in front of Caroline, shielding her from the creep's view.

The guy, obviously taken aback, glanced at the tree and then at Riley. "Were you up there the whole time?"

Riley shrugged nonchalantly. "I dunno. Maybe, maybe not. That's not the point. The point is the lady said to leave her alone." Despite his heart thudding like crazy at this guy's glower, Riley put on a brave face and waved his hand dismissively. "Come on, Caroline." Riley took her arm and started for the school building. He left cheek suddenly tickled. *What in—! 'Guess it's an ant! Must've gotten on me while I was in the tree.* He swiped the back of his hand across his face. Hmm. Odd. Nothing there.

"Hang on just a minute." The guy snagged Riley by the shoulder, grabbing a fistful of his shirt and turned him around. "What're you, some guardian angel? You've got a lot of nerve, swooping in like that and telling me to go."

Riley pulled away from the guy's hold, whose eyes flashed vehemently. Riley took a step back, choosing his words carefully. "Look, Caroline told you to leave her alone. Why not just ask out someone else?"

The guy seemed dangerously on the verge of attacking Riley as his glower deepened and his eyes turned dark. Riley fought the urge to back away. *Okay. That's creepy.*

"What? You gonna act like a knight in shining armor for them as well?" The guy lifted his fist.

"Felix!"

The guy—Felix—went pale, and his eyes immediately returned to normal.

"Mr. Davis!" Felix straightened as the principal, looking none too happy, stared him down.

Mr. Davis turned his gaze on Riley and then fixed it back on to Felix. "What're you doing? You're not hurting anyone, I hope? You know what happens if you attack a student one more time. Suspension."

When Felix peered down at Riley, Riley spotted shadows of hatred in his eyes. The shadows came and left in a rush. "Nothing, sir," Felix muttered.

Mr. Davis narrowed his eyes. He tilted his head at Riley. "Mr. McClinton? Is everything alright?"

Riley wanted to admit the truth to Mr. Davis, but what if this Felix guy came after him later when the principal wasn't around? "Yes, sir." He pasted on a smile, wishing he could wipe that smirk creeping over Felix's face.

"Mr. Brighton," the principal said, addressing Felix. "This is your last warning. Don't let me catch you trying to threaten anyone else."

Felix inclined his head. "Yes, sir."

"Now, go to class." The principal walked past them. Riley

heard Mr. Davis greet Caroline. Afterward, she made eye contact with Riley.

"Are you okay?"

Riley nodded, feeling the buzz on his cheek near his eye a second time. He attempted to ignore it as he responded, "Yeah. I'm fine. You?"

Caroline gave him a half-smile. "Yeah, I'm good. Thanks for helping me." With that, she headed for the school building. Riley went over to the tree to grab his lunchbox. Once again, the strange, tingling sensation continued. Riley brushed his eye with his knuckle. As he reached down for his lunchbox, Felix came out from behind the tree.

"Whoa! Agh!" Riley yelped and hit his head against a low-hanging branch, clacking his teeth together. He didn't realize Felix hadn't gone in yet.

"You might want to watch yourself, McClinton," Felix hissed. The shadows in his gaze returned, making his eyes appear even more vindictive. "You think you're safe? Not by a long shot. You'll be in for some pain soon."

Riley, clenching his teeth and rubbing his head, looked at Felix through one eye. Gathering courage, he replied, "Hey, man. Mr. Davis said that you'd be suspended if you did anything else."

Felix covered the ground between them—his mouth twisting into an icy sneer. Riley pressed his back to the tree, wishing the principal would come out of the school building. "I know that, punk! I'm not dumb! Someday, though, I *will* get back at you. Today, I almost got in trouble *because of you*." Felix prodded Riley in the chest with his forefinger. "Next time, you won't be so lucky."

Riley wanted to remind Felix that he had put himself in trouble but who knew how far that would push Felix before he disregarded the principal's threat and beat Riley up? He could only hope this whole mess would soon be forgotten.

* * *

The next day, Riley made for the tree, hoping to get in some reading time before class started.

"Hey, dork! Whatcha in a hurry for?"

Riley stopped abruptly. Not Felix! *Oh, come on! Keep going!* He paused. *Hey. That wasn't Felix's voice. Eh, just keep going. Maybe whoever it is isn't even talking to me.* The incident from yesterday came back to Riley in full force. Since then, he'd managed to avoid Felix, but Riley feared it would only be a matter of time before he ran into the guy again.

Riley jerked backward as a hand snatched his collar from behind.

Who in the—?

The moment he saw the face, Riley recognized it. Bryan Farmer—a tall, lanky, sandy-haired seventeen-year-old boy with lazy green eyes.

"Hey, fellas. Look who it is," Bryan said to four other boys, who, like Bryan, seemed to have come from out of nowhere. As he spoke, Bryan shook Riley like a ragdoll. Riley held his head, trying to keep himself from getting dizzy.

Bryan forced him to the center of the gang's circle. Feeling defiant, Riley stared at the ground, wishing Bryan would just leave. "What?" Bryan shook him some more. "Too scared to look at us? I'm not going to be ignored by a loser like you!"

Riley stopped clutching his head. Instead, he glared up at the boy, who finally stopped shaking him.

Bryan laughed. "That's more like it! So, as I was saying, whatcha in a hurry for, *dork*?"

Riley tried to remain calm. To his relief, the school bell

rang. Unfortunately, Bryan wasn't the least bit fazed. "Dude, what the heck? Lemme go! What're you doing? I have to get to class, as do you. We're gonna be late."

Bryan grinned, but the smile didn't reach his eyes. "It's your fault, loser. Besides, *you*"—he poked his forefinger into Riley's chest—"Came out here instead of staying inside. Should've thought twice!"

"What do you care what I do?" Riley ground out through his teeth. "Look, man. I've *gotta* go to class. Now, let. Me. *Go*!"

Bryan's eyes flashed. Riley groaned. Seriously—first Felix, now Bryan?! Two bullies coming after him just a day after each other. Bryan's attention, however, suddenly switched to another boy. The new kid, Max Jefferson, whose lean build and brown hair reminded Riley of his own. Max struggled to keep his backpack upright while running to the school's front door.

A twisted smile slowly formed on Bryan's face. He released Riley and headed to the other boy. The new kid stopped once Bryan caught up to him.

Riley bit his lip. *No! He'll only slow you down! Run!* Max seemed as though he wanted to avoid Bryan, but Bryan barred his way, forcing him to stay put.

The rest of the gang glanced at Riley before joining Bryan.

Seeing his chance, Riley made for the building, wincing when he heard Bryan pull Max's backpack off and rip open the zipper, despite Max's protests. When he peered back, Bryan had pushed Max and dumped everything out of his backpack.

Riley clenched his fists, but what could he do? If he stood up to Bryan, who knew what would happen? Making his way inside, Riley couldn't shake the feeling of cowardice overwhelming him like an illness.

During the day, Riley heard about how Bryan tormented the new kid. Though relieved Bryan's sights were set off of him, Riley didn't feel any better that someone else was the new target. Later, as Riley walked down the hallway, he witnessed Bryan shoving Max into the lockers.

Riley's face grew hot with anger. He stood still as conflict raged within him, kindling something in his chest.

He needed to help Max.

His head screamed, *Are you insane? You've managed to stay safe from Felix. What's the matter with you?!* He ignored it. Marching over to Bryan, Riley pushed him aside—albeit nervously—as sweat beaded his forehead. "Come on, man! Leave him alone!"

Bryan looked at him, surprised. "What?" Once he recovered, he narrowed his eyes. Riley sucked in a sharp breath, knowing the trouble he was getting himself into, but refused to back down. "You think you're so tough?" Bryan shoved Riley hard into the wall, winding him, with one hand gripping Riley's backpack strap. "You're *nothing* but a little wimp! Ya got that?"

For a moment, Riley feared Bryan would beat him up right there. His heart sped up double-time.

Bryan's resentful gaze seemed to drill straight through him. Riley's desire to look down fought against his anger. Eventually, after a minute or so passed without Riley relenting, Bryan released the strap and simply walked away.

"Thanks, man," Max smiled.

Riley gave him a brief nod. He knew, however, that Bryan wasn't finished with him, yet.

When he arrived at history class, Bryan—walking right behind Riley—pushed him into someone else's desk, earning Riley an irritated scowl from the other student. No point trying to blame Bryan. "Out of my way, loser," Bryan hissed. Riley grunted but didn't say anything. "Not such a tough guy after all, eh?" Bryan sneered once Riley sat down. "Keep in mind, punk—you're not brave enough to stand up to me!"

Riley said nothing. Acknowledging the statement would

only give Bryan satisfaction. But as Riley watched Bryan and his gang take their seats and talk amongst themselves, the strange sensation came over him from earlier. The tickle. Riley, aggravated, scratched at his face. *Go away!* Perhaps it was a gnat that'd followed him inside.

Bryan passed notes to his buddies during class, and they chuckled while making sure the teacher didn't overhear them. Of course, no one dared snitch on them. A crinkling sound pulled Riley's attention to a piece of paper that had fallen beside his desk. Glancing at the teacher and then at Bryan, he picked it up and unfolded the note. "*Max showed me up in math yesterday. Not cool! That guy's going down! After that—*"

Bryan had drawn an evil smiley face at the end of the sentence.

Not if I can help it! Riley balled his fists and turned his glower on Bryan, who—noticing Riley had read the note—only leaned back in his chair, arms folded, and smirked, daring him to do something about it. Riley grumbled as he turned away, attempting to focus on the whiteboard. A derisive chuckle mocked him from behind.

You're not brave enough! Bryan's accusation repeated in his mind.

We'll see about that. Somehow.

Chapter Two

Later that day, Riley mulled over possible ways he could keep out of trouble—while helping Max. There had to be a way. Bryan needed to get a life and stop picking on others! Needless to say, his cousin needed to quit as well. Riley rounded the corner on the way to his next class, when a noise made him lift his head. Bryan stood next to the doorway to the cafeteria. Heart stuttering fearfully, Riley whipped back around the corner and pressed himself against the red brick wall. So much for wanting to do something about his fear. Thankfully, the cafeteria entrance was far enough away from the corner where Riley hid so that Bryan wouldn't have heard him. However, Riley did hear a voice, and it wasn't Bryan's. He'd hid so fast he didn't notice anyone else there.

He peeked around the edge, and his eyes went wide. Felix! He stood before Bryan with a cold frown. Felix seemed to have Bryan trapped at the lockers. One of the oversized cafeteria doors—blocking any prying eyes from immediately looking around the corner—offered convenient hiding. Bryan's own cousin, trapping and glowering at him, as though intending to beat him up? Where were Bryan's buds? Riley glanced over his shoulder just to make sure they weren't there, ready to pounce.

Besides, didn't Bryan have a class going on right now?

. . . Besides, didn't he, Riley, also have a class going on right now?

"You didn't bother doing anything to him, eh, buddy-boy?" Riley heard Felix say, his voice laced with a snide touch, catching Riley's attention. *Buddy-boy*? What was this, a cartoon?

Riley thought he saw Bryan's throat move, as if swallowing. Did Felix scare him that badly? Taking a good look—or, at least, as good a look as he could, being a short distance away—Riley noted how Felix's fists tightened to the point of his veins popping out. The menace in his glare, evident. What was up with this guy?

"No, I didn't," Bryan muttered. "I don't care about what he does anyway. I plan to only focus on Max. He showed me up in class. If you want to do anything about it, then you do it." What were they talking about?

Felix closed in on Bryan—practically nose-to-nose with him. Bryan pressed against the brick wall. Riley's gut lurched. Felix wasn't planning on attacking Bryan, was he? Bryan must've feared the same as he leaned his head back to the wall. "I told you I'd be suspended if I made any moves. I don't care if you don't want to do anything about him." Felix poked his finger into Bryan's chest. "If you do nothing, you'll look like a *coward.* I told you that if you didn't *beat,*" (poke) "him up, then I would tell *everyone,*" (poke) "in our family about *your little incident.*" He added three extra pokes with the last three words.

What little incident?

"And do to you what I do to him."

"Felix—"

"Shut up!" Felix grabbed Bryan by his jacket lapels. He didn't lift Bryan towards him, but he did push him into the wall.

Riley gawked. *What in the world?* His eyes hurt from keeping them open for so long, but he didn't want to leave, as he wanted to see what Bryan would do. He blinked a few times to moisten them and released a breath he didn't know he'd been holding.

"Listen. If you don't want anyone to know what you did to Gavin and Jack, then I recommend you make up for it right now, buddy-boy," Felix admonished. His calm tone sent shivers down Riley's spine. Then, for a moment, there was silence. "McClinton ran into me just today. Need I remind you, the guy who stole my chance with Caroline Fairburn? *You're* the only one who can nail him for me."

Riley's face lost all feeling.

"If you want me to forget what you did to Gavin and Jack, *you* have to take that McClinton guy out if he bothers us again. Besides, you don't just let a chump like him get in the way of you getting at dorks like that Max kid." Felix stopped suddenly. "Wait. Max corrected you *in class*!? Nerds like him don't get off easily with something like that. You want to focus on Max? I'll cover for you, but you need to take out that Riley kid first. Remember, Brye, I'm just trying to help ya. You don't want me to tell Uncle Les what happened? Do you?"

Riley had heard enough. Bryan muttered something, but Riley had no interest in hearing the response. Tormented by his cousin. Was that why he acted the way he did? It would make sense! Nevertheless, Felix wanted Bryan to pulverize Riley for him. Riley didn't realize it at first, but his legs were shaking. He also tasted blood in his mouth. He'd bitten down on his tongue without realizing it. Riley touched his temple, feeling sweat. Surprisingly, he felt somewhat bad for Bryan. Bryan was a bully, but Riley didn't expect to see the bully being bullied by someone else. And worse, by his own cousin! Yet, if Riley tried to stand up to Felix, who knew what can of worms that would open?

To take his mind off of the conversation, he directed his focus on his class. Tardy or not, he pushed away from the wall, being as quiet as possible, and took the long route. He needed to help Max. Keep him safe. He would need to be around Max throughout the day—even though, that would prove a challenge. Another thing—Bryan's words echoed in his head about him not being brave. Did Bryan say that, as he felt that way himself?

Riley got into the classroom and apologized to the teacher for being late. His teacher cocked a brow, and muttered something about students and tardiness before continuing with the lesson. Riley didn't hear the rebuke as he concentrated on figuring out ways to keep from being nailed by Bryan. *"If you don't want anyone to know what you did to Gavin and Jack, then I recommend you make up for it right now. If you want me to forget what you did to Gavin and Jack, you have to take that McClinton guy out."*

An hour later, Riley looked both ways before leaving the classroom and headed to the cafeteria. Hopefully, Max would be there, too. And safe.

"Riley!"

"Caroline?"

His friend came sprinting up and paused to catch her breath. She pointed down the hall. "Bryan has Max! I saw them in the cafeteria."

Clenching his teeth, Riley bolted in that direction. He halted outside the cafeteria doors and saw Bryan with Max's shirt in his fist. Without a second thought, Riley shouted, "Bryan!"

Bryan paled as he whipped his head in Riley's direction, clearly expecting to see a teacher or administrator. Upon seeing Riley, however, his eyes went from terrified to incensed. Snarling, he released Max and came for his new victim. "Gonna be brave now, huh?" Numb with a more palpable dread, Riley dashed back the way he'd come. The few students hanging around didn't question the kid running past like his life depended on it. Which it sort of did. Taking a chance, Riley rushed into one of the open classrooms. Thankfully, it was empty. He placed his back to the open door, putting himself between the whiteboard and the door.

He heard Bryan huffing. Riley pursed his lips. He hoped Bryan would continue his search down the hall. Unfortunately, to his dismay, footsteps stopped in the doorway. Riley forced himself to keep from swallowing, as he believed the smallest sound could catch Bryan's attention. The guy had some sharp ears. Riley's heart drummed, and he slowly moved his hand to it, attempting to calm it down. *Please, God. Please. Please, no.* He could hear Bryan walk into the room. Riley's stomach soured. Sweat dripped down his chin, and one bead trickled into his eye. *Ack!* Riley fought to keep from rubbing it. *God, no. Don't let him look over here,* he begged. The footsteps paused for a moment . . . and then they left. Riley gulped, hard. He placed his hands on the whiteboard, catching his breath, and attempted to calm himself down. Why Bryan didn't think to check behind the door was beyond Riley, although he didn't speculate on the question for long. No need to.

I can't live my life as a coward. I won't. No matter what it costs. Riley clenched his fists. *The next person I see being bullied, I'm going to do something about it! I'm going to bring this all to an end.*

Even if it's Felix bullying Bryan? The thought came to him, unbidden. He nodded to himself, albeit, hesitantly. *Even if.*

Riley raced from the classroom, hoping to avoid an early death in case Bryan was nearby. He didn't spot Max anywhere and hoped the new boy was already in class. Thankfully, Riley's classroom was just around the corner up ahead. It hadn't started yet when he arrived, and neither Felix nor Bryan were in this class with him. Sitting at his desk, Riley took out his notebook and wrote, *"Priority #1 – next person I see bullied, I'm going to help them."* Riley felt his classmates staring at him. Did they know about the skirmish going on between him, Felix, Bryan, and Max?

Once class finished, Riley went into the hall and scanned the area for Max. Students crowded the foyer, making it nearly impossible to spot any particular person. Eventually, it cleared enough for Riley to hear a scuffling sound close by. Down the hall, Felix's tall form stood by Max's locker.

"We're the welcoming committee, man," Felix said, "and we wanna get to know you better."

Max's eyes widened as Felix forced him towards the doors leading outside. Though he struggled to get away, his physique was nothing compared to Felix's. Riley's gut grew cold. The halls emptied for the most part. A few students still milled about, but no one seemed interested in giving Max a hand.

Forget Felix and Bryan's threats! Straightening his shoulders, Riley took a deep breath and made for the doors.

Stepping outside, he noticed Felix standing close by. *Agh!* Riley paid him no heed as he located Bryan just in time to see him push Max to the ground.

"Not surprised you'd show up!" Felix said—tone dripping

with contempt. Riley glared at Felix out of the corner of his eye, then focused his attention on Max.

"Quit it, guys!" Max exclaimed, trying to grab his glasses out of Bryan's hand. Bryan threw them on the ground and stomped on them. Riley gasped. "What the heck was *that* for?!" Max said, looking ready to fight Bryan. The kid was small for his age and Bryan easily shoved him to the ground.

"Bryan!" Riley shouted. Max whipped around. Bryan lifted his head. The same apprehension from earlier when hearing his name, shone in his eyes for a split second before he realized who'd spoken. "Look who just arrived, guys," he sneered. "McClinton."

Riley helped Max up. "You okay, man?"

Max pointed at Bryan and then at his glasses. "That jerk just broke my glasses! Who does that?"

Riley glared at Bryan. "This is *not* cool, man! What's your deal?" Again, he felt that strange, tingling sensation around his left eye.

"Oooh, gonna be a tough guy now, eh? What're you gonna do about it? Huh?" Bryan closed in on him, eyes glinting. Riley stepped back. Hmm. Would Felix have been more preferable? "You're not strong enough to take me on. You're not strong enough to take any of us on!" Bryan and his gang formed a circle around Riley and Max.

"Who'll take the first beating?"

Riley had to figure out something, and fast.

"Well, losers. Who'll it be?" Bryan demanded, lifting his fist.

Out of the corner of his eye, Riley noticed Felix watching with, what appeared to be intense interest. Felix, no doubt, put Bryan up to this. Riley caught a glimpse of the principal walking into the school building, and an idea came to him—

though it was super risky. He could run to the principal's office and let him know what Bryan was doing.

It seemed Bryan read his mind, for he grabbed Riley by the forefront of his shirt. "Don't even think about it, McClinton! Or else."

With all his might, Riley pushed Bryan out of the way and dashed to the building.

"Don't just stand there, you idiots!" Bryan shouted. "Get him!"

Riley didn't bother looking back as he ran. Footsteps neared behind him, and when he reached the door, a hand snatched his collar.

In a panic—thinking it was Felix—Riley jerked his elbow back. It connected, causing the other boy to let go. Panting, Riley pulled the door open. A spike of pain surged through his shoulder as it hit the door's edge. The handful of students remaining watched him, stunned and curious. He sprinted to the principal's office, yelling, "Mr. Davis!"

The principal turned to Riley, eyes wide. "Mr. McClinton! What is the matter?"

Riley bent over, catching his breath. "Bryan . . . he—" Riley paused as his brain screamed, *Don't do it! Bryan'll kill you for sure!* Riley felt the stares of the people around him. "Bryan, he . . . he . . ." Riley trailed off. Would it be worth telling the principal what happened, especially with other kids around?

Mr. Davis cocked a brow. "Bryan? As in, Bryan Farmer?"

"Y-yes, sir," Riley nodded, gulping in air. A part of him wanted to forget everything he'd witnessed. Forget the risk he'd put himself in. Convincing himself he couldn't turn back anyway, Riley shoved those protests aside. "Bryan broke Max's glasses. He stomped on them and pushed Max down."

Mr. Davis didn't say anything for a minute or two. The only

sign for his thoughts was the disapproval in his eyes. The silence, laden with suspense, gave Riley knots in his stomach and the strange buzz returned. Eventually, the principal called out to the Dean of Students across the hall. "Please bring in Mr. Farmer and his friends, as well as Max Jefferson. Thank you."

Riley's forehead perspired. "Umm, sir? Can I go home now?" Riley wanted to get out before Bryan had an opportunity to catch him. He knew what would happen if he remained here with Bryan and his gang when the principal and vice–principal left.

"You are a witness, Mr. McClinton. We need you to explain what you saw," the principal replied.

God, why? Why did he have to be the one to help Max? Why couldn't someone else have done it? Despite being bullied by Bryan for the past several years, Riley had never stood up to the guy. Riley knew the consequences. Bryan had threatened him from day one—"Mess with me, and you're dead." He'd been shoved, laughed at, called names, but never in *this* situation. *You know I've tried so hard to keep out of trouble. Why didn't You help me this time?*

A small whisper brushed past his ear. *"Consider Bryan and his situation."*

Huh? What does that mean? Who said that?

The cool breeze blowing from the air conditioner only served to increase the numbness enveloping him.

Bryan and his gang walked into the room, glowering at Riley with unveiled hatred. Particularly Bryan. Max, who held his broken glasses, stood alongside the Dean of Students. Too afraid to even glance to the side, Riley didn't need to look at Bryan to know how the guy felt towards him right now. Like a weight pressing down on Riley's chest, the air seemed to dissipate in the room.

"Mr. Farmer. Mr. McClinton here says you *broke* Max Jefferson's glasses? You did this on purpose?"

Bryan didn't say anything for a few seconds, until he muttered, "Yes, sir. It's true. But I promise it will not happen again. I was . . . mad. So, I took my anger out on Max." Much to Riley's confusion (and amazement), Bryan looked at Max and apologized. It even sounded genuine, as though he truly was sorry. Max reacted with no less astonishment than Riley. Once he found the words to speak, Max gave Bryan a small smile and murmured, "We're good, man."

However, when Bryan peered at Riley, his eyes glinted. Great. Apparently, he was far from through where Riley was concerned.

"Bryan Farmer, you will be suspended for the rest of this week. We will not tolerate violence in this facility."

Ringing pulsed in Riley's ears and his body turned ice–cold. When he returned to school on Monday, no doubt Felix, Bryan, and the gang would be waiting for him.

Yep, he might as well go ahead and count himself dead.

As the principal turned to speak to the Dean of Students, Riley's shirt collar seemed to tighten under Bryan's scorching gaze.

Riley finally dared a peek at Bryan, who slid a finger across his throat and then pointed the finger straight at him. Tugging at his collar and gulping hard, Riley tried to settle the fear building up inside. Max, not seeing this exchange, smiled gratefully at Riley. *At least someone's happy.*

"You are dismissed, Mr. McClinton. I will call Mr. Jefferson's parents to notify them of the incident. Mr. Farmer? I want to talk to you for a little while longer. I want to know of your motives for breaking Max's glasses. Plus, your history teacher has some questions for you."

Riley, more than happy to oblige, left the office as hastily as possible, but not before one of the guys in Bryan's gang—a tall, freckled kid with wild, red-orange hair—hissed in his ear, "We're gonna destroy you later, hero-boy."

Ignoring the comment, Riley walked on by, wishing to sink into the floor and forget that entire day. Upon leaving the building, he tried to focus on the schoolwork he needed to do when he got home, but his jangled nerves didn't lessen. The school bus had already gone, of course, but he didn't want to ride the bus, even if he could. His stomach tightened to the point of feeling sick. The back of his neck prickled with heat.

Pursing his lips, Riley eyed his surroundings. *Something is definitely wrong.* He quickened his pace. The street was too quiet. Unsettling.

"Got 'im!"

A hand latched onto his bag and yanked him backward. Riley yelped and landed on the ground with a thud. When he opened his eyes, Bryan's gang stood there. "Wait! But . . . you guys were still in the principal's office!"

The largest of Bryan's cronies stepped closer. Riley scrambled back. Their anger was tangible and he wanted to run if they started to attack. "Mr. Davis let us out. Bryan's about here."

Bryan's . . . about . . . shoot! Riley made to leave, but they formed a circle around him. The big guy scowled fiercely. "Bryan's not gonna letchu get away with this, punk! You know that, right?"

Before Riley could speak, a voice laced with fury snarled, "Oh, he knows it all right!"

Oh, come on!

They parted, giving Bryan an opening. "I told you to watch yourself, or you'd be dead, didn't I? As a matter of fact, since day one, I said you'd be a goner if you messed with me. Guess you're too stupid to listen."

A couple of the guys grabbed Riley's arms and pinned them behind his back.

Riley pushed and pulled, attempting to wriggle out of their grasp, but to no avail. "Speaking of stupid—Bryan, just because Max Jefferson corrected you in class doesn't give you the right to break his glasses! That's just the most ridiculous thing anyone could do!"

Bryan's eyelids lowered halfway over his eyes. Riley knew this look. It'd always been one of the ways Bryan expressed anger. He'd seen it in class whenever someone upped Bryan. "You know, you could've saved yourself the trouble and let someone else take the beating. Instead, you had to mess everything up for yourself, didntcha?" Bryan—similar to what Felix did to him—stood directly in front of Riley and stared him down. "I have to admit, Riley, I'm actually surprised by you. You snitched on me to the principal. For a while there, you didn't have the guts to fight back. Do you have the guts to take on *all* of us?"

"*Oolf*!" Bryan's fist drove full force into Riley's gut, chasing the air from his lungs. Riley collapsed to his knees, keeping a tight grip on his stomach. He coughed, working to take in all the breath he could muster while the pain spread through his midsection.

Bryan had not wasted any energy with his blow.

"Let this teach you something, dork. If you snitch on me ever again, I will beat the living daylights out of you! Ya know?" Bryan paused. "Come to think of it, why wait?"

As soon as he could breathe, Riley spat out, "I would do it again if I had to."

The strange, tingling sensation returned, much stronger now. When Riley lifted his head, Bryan and his gang immediately shuffled away, staring at him as if he had suddenly grown an extra limb. Their faces went white, and they moved even further back as he stood.

Riley cocked a brow. "What is it with you guys?" Was that actual panic in Bryan's eyes? "Stop staring. You guys are making me feel weird." When they didn't answer, Riley shrugged and plodded off in the direction of his house. The pain in his gut had lessened, but took a lot out of him, so he didn't have the energy to run.

What had freaked those guys out, anyway?

Chapter Three

Riley hefted his backpack and squared his shoulders, then walked through town, ignoring the people he passed, desperately hoping to steer clear of attention. Why had Bryan and his gang stared at him in such terror?

The fewer people from school who saw him and the fewer questions asked, the better. He kept his head low, thankful that not many people were out and about.

"Hey, Riley!"

He bit back a sigh as a group of friends from school approached from the crosswalk.

"Did you seriously snitch on Bryan? What happened? Man, I can't believe you did that," one of the kids exclaimed.

Riley's neck grew hot under his shirt, but he resisted pulling at it. News traveled fast around here.

"Dude!" one of the guys said. "Do you have a bruise or something? Did Bryan hit you in the eye?"

"It's shaped like a star!" One of the girls pointed at Riley's eye.

Riley held up his hands and shook his head. "W–what're you talking about? What star?"

The girl came closer. "*That*!" she said, nearly touching Riley's face. Did she know anything about personal space? "It's a star."

"What . . ." He glanced in a window next to him and did a double–take. "What in . . .?"

He leaned in, blinking several times. Starting at the center of his left eye and stretching halfway across it, was the outline a star. A black star, right there. "Where did—?"

Riley jerked back when a man on the other side of the window looked at him in confusion.

"You alright, kiddo?" The store owner popped his head out the door. "This fella here says you freaked out when you looked inside. Something wrong?" He squinted. "Is that a star on your face?"

Riley panted, unable to answer. He couldn't figure out what to say!

"Is everything okay, son?" a policeman—who also happened to be in the store—inquired. "Not causing trouble, are you?" Even though the question was meant as a joke, Riley backed off, as if he were a criminal.

"Ahh! It must be a tattoo!" one of the guys from school exclaimed.

Huh? Riley's mind spun. "A tattoo? I dunno *where* this thing came from, but it sure as heck is not a tattoo!"

The group of teens looked at each other doubtfully. "Are you sure?" one of the guys asked.

Riley clutched his head. "It's not a tattoo!"

He kept his head down, but people on the streets still stared at him. Apparently, the star was more noticeable than he realized. He had to find a place to think and look at the star.

Seeing an empty alleyway, Riley ducked in and hid beside

a pile of cement slabs. He took out his phone, opened the camera, and inspected the star. Brushing his wavy brown hair out of the way, Riley narrowed his eyes at the camera.

It wasn't terribly big, but it sure was obvious. He held his forefinger up parallel to his eye to measure the star. It stretched from the tip of his forefinger to about the middle. Another thing. What about the strange tickle he'd been feeling all day? Did that have anything to do with the star? How could it? The star just appeared out of nowhere. The most important question, on the other hand—where did it come from??

His phone read 4:30 p.m. He had to get home soon. What would his parents say when they saw it?

Caroline's name popped up on the screen. He swiped to answer.

"Hey," she said. "What's up? You okay? Did Bryan and his gang come after you?"

"Yeah . . . the worst that happened was Bryan punching me in the gut. Otherwise, I'm fine." Riley groaned. "There's a . . . a star on my eye."

"What? When did—wait, what?"

"There—look, this is gonna sound weird, but there is a star on my eye, and I have no earthly idea how it got there and what to do about it!" He ended the call.

What am I doing? What am I gonna do? What can I do?

Riley sat there for half an hour, trying to sort through his options. The shadows grew longer. A breeze passed through the alley, chilling him.

"Riley? What're you doing here?"

Riley's head shot up, and he spotted Caroline standing at the opposite wall.

"I . . . wait, how did you find me?"

She pointed at his phone. "I saw the light from your phone,

and it was shining on your face. Whoa! Is *that* the star? Where did it come from?"

Riley shrugged. "I don't know. I'm just trying to hide until I figure out what to do."

Caroline tilted her head. "Well, you can't hide it for long, y'know?"

Her statement sent a shudder through his body. Dismissing it, Riley spread out his palms. "I'm not sure what to do. I don't know how to explain it, but I have this weird tingly, tickly feeling in my eye, sort of like a bug crawling on my face." Caroline grimaced. "I first noticed it when I helped Max Jefferson. I guess that's when the star showed up. But now—" he paused and pointed to the star, "I wanna hide this thing before it causes any trouble."

Caroline shook her head. "Well, as I said, you can't hide it for long."

Why did a chill creep into Riley's heart at that last comment?

"I . . . I know." What else was there to say? Following a slightly awkward pause, Caroline took some sort of makeup stuff out of her backpack and handed it to him. "Put it on. It's concealer and it might help."

Concealer? Riley spread it on his eye, using his phone for light, trying to avoid touching it. The concealer felt cold. but it hid the star somewhat. Unless someone looked closely, they wouldn't see it. Hopefully. "Maybe the concealer will work somehow." Caroline's phone bleeped. After checking it, she said, "Hey, I need to go. Supper's ready." She paused. "Text me if you need any help!"

Riley smiled. "Thanks."

Caroline sprinted off, leaving Riley to observe on his camera how much the star showed through the concealer. The concealer didn't hide it very well, but it wasn't totally discernable.

Pushing himself up, Riley finally headed home. He'd seen Caroline's unease. She didn't know what to think, and he didn't blame her. He didn't know what to think, either. Wanting to avoid any more curious glances, Riley hid in the forest.

It was 5:00 p.m. now, and his parents would be expecting him home. *I can't go home. Not yet!*

Riley sat between two trees, above a little ridge, and leaned against one of them. "What do I tell my parents?" he sighed. "I could tell them I got punched in the eye . . ."

Yeah, Riley sneered at himself, *that'll totally explain the star–shaped bruise.* "What in the world do I tell them?" He thumped his head a couple of times on the tree, in the hope that an idea would suddenly materialize.

"I understand your situation."

Riley's eyes flew open. He jumped to his feet and stared at his surroundings, trying to seek out the owner of the voice, which had an Irish accent. "Who—? Who said that?"

The voice was quiet for a minute or two. When it spoke again, it sounded nearer. "My name is John Alan O'Shea, but I am called Alan. I over'eard your situation."

Riley's stomach clenched to realize someone had been listening to him. He narrowed his eyes and didn't move. The trees swayed in the breeze. A couple of birds chirped. A chill crept up his spine. Had someone from Bryan's gang followed him into the forest? "A-are you hiding?"

"No."

Riley glanced around, and then climbed a few feet up the ridge to see if the individual could, perchance, be higher than him. There was not a single soul in sight. "Why can't I see you?"

"You probably don't see me because you are not yet ready to see me."

Huh? Riley peeked over his shoulder, leery. "'Not yet ready'? What's that supposed to mean?"

"You can 'ear me, but you cannot see where I am. Why, I am standing right in front of you!"

Freezing in his steps, Riley stared at the spot before him. *Right in front of me?* The only things in sight were trees, a sloping hill, bushes, and a little bit of the town through the leaves.

"I—"

A liquid form appeared. A bluish-white figure that looked like a man. A man with a slightly frayed robe, a balding head, and a kind smile.

Riley staggered back, dumbfounded, and strangely giddy. He gasped, "You–you're–you're a . . . a gh-a gho—!" Prickles filled his body from the balls of his feet to his palms and he lost his footing. The forest spun as Riley somersaulted backward down the hill. His stomach flipped, threatening to lose its contents.

"Augh!" His head thudded against the ground, and a blanket of darkness overtook him.

"Riley." The voice was distant but clear.

"Riley."

Riley slowly opened his eyes. The ghost, Alan, stood—floated?—above him. A surge of pain lanced through the back of Riley's neck, and his head smarted from the fall. Thankfully, nothing seemed to be broken. "Ow." As he sat up, Riley winced and narrowed his eyes at Alan. "Okay, so . . . I would say that hitting my head is causing me to see you, but that can't be right because I saw you before I fell." He rubbed his head, amazed that he was otherwise unharmed.

The ghost chuckled. It didn't sound mocking. Good-natured would be a better description. "I daresay it is not the case! Are you alright?"

Riley glared at him.

"Forgive me. Wrong question. Any bumps, bruises, or scratches?"

Riley checked himself but found none. "No. Just hurt my head."

Alan knelt next to him, scanning his face and shoulders. Riley, inadvertently, sidled away. If Alan noticed, he didn't say anything.

"Are you sure? You seem quite dazed."

"Well, I *did* just fall. I also know this has to be my imagination. You can't be real. You're a ghost, for Pete's sake! Ghosts aren't real! Besides, how do you know my name?"

Alan squinted one of his eyes. "I am indeed a ghost. I'm glad you figured that out. In my past life, I 'ailed from Ireland. I moved to the world of Leíso when I arrived 'ere as a 'uman. Zefa is the village where I lived in Leíso. As for the other question, Dorobonn told me your name."

"B-but, you can't be real," Riley stammered. Legs shaking, he stood back up. "This is only my imagination. Wait, who's Dorobonn?"

"Your imagination? Oh, I can tell you for a fact that I am not a figment of your imagination. Quite the opposite! In fact, if you think *I'm* an illusion, you might very well 'ave difficulty taking in what I'm about to tell you."

A wave of uncertainty engulfed Riley, suffocating him.

Alan pointed a misty finger at his chest. "You, young man, are a part of a legend that spans for 'undreds of years. You see, the star you 'ave is a symbol."

"Wait! You know about my star?! Can you tell me where it came from?" So much for the concealer.

Alan looked around as though making sure no one could overhear them. "Aye. You are not the first one to 'ave gotten a star. There was someone else before you, but they did not live to fulfill the prophecy. Neither did the one before them."

Riley didn't like the direction Alan was going with this. "Prophecy? W-what"—he gulped—"happened to them?"

"They both died. But it is not my place to tell you 'ow they died or of your place in the legend. Dorobonn informed me about you, and 'e will be the one to explain everything."

Riley's dizziness returned. "There you go again with that name. Dorobonn. Who's that?"

"Ah, yes! Apologies. 'e is a magician, Dorobonn is. A powerful one, too. 'e focuses on Light Magic." Alan looked up at the sky as if this Dorobonn guy would come down from there. "But, as I said, it is not my place to tell you everything. I only came to tell you that you are a part of a prophecy and that, dear boy, is why your star 'as appeared. Once Dorobonn finds you, you will need to go through the door, the Door of Tranien leading into Leíso into the village of Zefa. The door is in this very forest, but you cannot find it unless you are prepared to see it—just as you were not prepared to see me, originally."

Wow . . . am I seriously starting to lose it? Door of Tranien? This couldn't be real.

Riley looked at his phone, almost unconscious of what he was doing. 6:00 p.m.! "Oh boy. My parents are gonna kill me! I need to leave." Not to mention, all of this information was about to make him go nuts.

Alan nodded slowly. "Very well. I best be off myself. Just remember to keep an eye out for Dorobonn. 'e will be 'ere shortly."

Riley clicked his tongue. "Okay. Got it! Wait, what does he look like?"

Alan's ghostly form dissolved as he answered, "You'll know! Believe me, you'll know! I will see you again, Riley."

Riley blinked, but Alan was gone.

Chapter Four

Riley trod carefully through the forest and back onto the road that led to his house. *Did I actually just meet a ghost? It mustn't have been real.* He also hoped supper wasn't ready yet. That would mean he'd still have enough time to make it . . . his phone vibrated. Squeezing his eyes shut and then reluctantly opening them, Riley took his phone out of his pocket and read the message from his mom.

- *Supper's been ready for the past 45 minutes. Where are you?*

He sucked in a sharp breath. Great. He typed back, *I was talking with Caroline Fairburn and lost track of time.*

Plausible.

He pressed send and continued up the road, his thoughts returning to the ghost.

How can I know if I'm not insane? I mean, okay, this star is obviously real. That's evident. But what about Alan? This door he mentioned? Especially this Dorobonn guy he spoke of.

Riley's head hurt from trying to figure everything out. He decided to put these questions on hold until after he ate.

As the sun sank behind the mountains, the pink and purple sky gave off its last bit of light for the evening. What other worlds hid beyond those mountains? Beyond his world? Was there another place he could go to find answers?

Other worlds? Where did he get that idea?

The strange prickly sensation near his eye that he'd felt earlier returned. *Okay, this feeling has come to me several times already. What is going on?* He considered the idea he'd dismissed earlier—*does it have anything to do with the star? What other explanation could there be?*

Riley glanced up through the trees. The moon shone bright and silver, with only one star visible. The cobalt hue of the vast sky stared down at him. Answers seemed so far away, yet . . .

As Riley reached the driveway, the lights in the house lit up in his peripheral and cast a glow through the windows, brightening up the porch. He chewed his lip. His mom hadn't texted back. Hopefully, that wasn't a bad sign.

He slowly walked up to the front door, both embarrassed and nervous to hear the scolding sure to follow his arrival.

Bracing himself, Riley took a deep breath and opened the door. When he entered the dining room, all eyes focused on him. His face grew hot. His mom raised her brows, the reprimand clear in her eyes. His dad looked back at his plate but didn't say anything. Terry and Braydon didn't speak. They immediately went back to eyeing their food as well. The dim light in the dining room must've hidden his star since they said nothing about it.

Wait, even if they hadn't mentioned it yet, could that necessarily mean they hadn't seen it?

His mom blinked several times as if confused. Braydon

slowly lifted his head and watched him, stunned. Not terrified, but stunned. Any hopes of them not seeing his star evaporated.

Riley sat at the table and kept his head down, hoping to appear chastised rather than fearful or concerned. He stared at the spaghetti in front of him, praying for a distraction.

His arm tickled as Braydon drew closer and closer to him.

"Huh?" he heard Braydon say.

"Do you mind?" Riley shot Braydon a glare, unintentionally giving them all an unmistakable view of his star.

"When did you get a tattoo?!" the thirteen–year–old exclaimed, his tone awfully close to that of whining.

If Riley didn't know any better, he'd think Braydon sounded jealous. His mind whirled and his palms started to sweat.

"Braydon," their father admonished in a stern tone—his head turned slightly towards the youngest boy, but his eyes remained fixed on Riley. "Son, when did you get a tattoo? Was that what you were doing earlier?"

Although it was not a tattoo, Riley scratched the back of his neck, searching for a good response.

"No, sir, it's not a tattoo. I'm telling you, it's not. Stop looking at me like that!" he snapped at Braydon, who seemed far more intrigued than made Riley comfortable.

"But it's right there on your eye! Are you sure you didn't get a tattoo?" Braydon asked.

"Yes! I can't even *get* a tattoo legally!" Riley stood, and his words sounded more desperate to his ears. "Please. You gotta believe me. I—"

"Son, we do not appreciate this," his dad said, prodding the table once with his forefinger as though for emphasis. "Why are you lying to us?"

Riley didn't know how to answer. He wouldn't lie about

this. How could he get his family to understand? "I'm not lying!"

"Sit down." His mom pointed at his chair.

Riley squeezed his fist, only then realizing how he'd clenched it while trying to defend himself. *What's happening?* Chastised, he plopped down into the chair, but it only made him feel vulnerable.

"We don't understand, Riley. Why do you feel like you should lie to us? This isn't like you. You're too young for a tattoo, and you know it," his father said.

"I'm surprised, too!" Terry remarked.

"He got a tattoo!" Braydon said in an announcer's voice, like he hadn't stated it several times already. "I want one!"

"Braydon!" his father warned.

Riley's heart slammed against his ribcage. A knot tightened in his stomach. He broke out into a cold sweat. Everyone's voices began to fade.

Am I about to pass out again?

"We'll have to have it removed," his mother said.

"What?" Riley shouted, his alarm breaking through the conversations and even caught him off guard.

His mother, following an awkward and astonished silence, replied, "Excuse me?"

"Err . . . sorry, I didn't mean to shout." It was too much. Riley's vision swam. "No, wait. I'm not lying. I dunno where this thing came from! It appeared after . . . after . . ."

Should he tell them the truth about Bryan punching him? It might be a long shot. "I got it after Bryan punched me!"

Quiet greeted him like an unwelcomed stranger. The dimly lit room felt claustrophobic.

"Bryan *punched* you?" his mother exclaimed.

"But that doesn't explain the star," his father stated, eyes widening. "Did you tell the principal that Bryan punched you?"

"No, sir." Riley's throat constricted at the thought of telling Mr. Davis. "I don't wanna bother with it. If Bryan finds out, he'll beat me up. Again. He slugged me in the gut after I told the principal what he'd done to the new kid, Max. He'd pushed Max to the ground and broke his glasses." Riley inwardly winced. *I've said too much!*

"Bryan hurt you and the new boy and broke his glasses? Good heavens!" his mother remarked. She placed her hand on his dad's. "We're glad you stood up for someone, but Bryan shouldn't get away with attacking you, too."

"Mom, I—"

"Son," his father interjected, "the principal needs to know. You will have to tell him. First, we'll get this star business straightened out."

They continued eating, but Riley found it hard to breathe. Bryan would not hesitate to kill him. No joke! Then there was Felix and it was impossible to predict what that guy would do if Riley encountered him again, which was inevitable. Not to mention he couldn't tell Mr. Davis about the incident. The more Riley puzzled through his options for getting around letting the principal know what happened, the farther he got from a solution.

Bryan.

Riley gulped hard. Simply remembering Bryan's anger was enough to make him queasy. Bryan was already facing suspension for the rest of the week. How would he react when he saw Riley again? With this star, who knew? Hopefully, it'd be gone by then . . .

The food didn't sit well with him anymore. Riley was exhausted. "I'm going upstairs. I don't feel good." Pushing from the table, Riley took his plate and cup to the sink and then headed for the stairs, not giving his parents any time to ask questions.

He opened his bedroom door, closed it quietly behind him, and then flopped onto his bed, allowing the cooling comfort of the blanket to take over his senses.

For twenty minutes, Riley laid on his bed, eyeing his collection of fantasy books on the shelf near his door. He never considered himself an actual fairy tale believer, but his imagination did take him places. Was that what this whole thing was? A figment of his imagination? Alan had said that he wasn't a part of Riley's imagination. Then again, would a person from his imagination say that? Plus, he had the star. Everyone could see it, which proved he wasn't going crazy. What if he hadn't actually woken up this morning? Maybe the ordeal he had experienced today was all just a part of one long dream?

His stomach growled. Never mind. The hunger he felt was real enough. The deafening silence in his room got to his brain. He didn't want to go downstairs and face more accusations or an avalanche of questions, but what else could he do? Who could help?

The name *Dorobonn* appeared in his mind.

Hmmm. How was he supposed to meet this guy?

Riley went to his window, pushed it up, and then climbed out. He needed to get out of the house to somewhere where he could think.

Scrambling down the tree right outside his room, he headed through the forest to his quiet place.

He lit up the growing dark with his phone, which read 8:00 p.m. What if his parents caught him? What if they were waiting for him when he came back? Was this a risk he was willing to take?

I need to find answers, somehow.

The late evening brought on a sense of calmness—a calmness Riley always felt when he walked in this forest. The moon brightened up the small opening in the trees where he sat. Shadows danced, making Riley's heart skip a beat.

Why am I so freaked out right now? His stomach cramped. Perhaps it was all the goings on from today which had increased his anxiety.

He listened for anything—or anyone—who might be around. Perspiration beaded his body. Sweat covered his fingers as he scratched his collar.

Riley wiped his face, wondering if Caroline's concealer had rubbed off on his hand.

He sensed something disconcerting in the air. Clenching his teeth, Riley slowly got to his feet. He would come back in the morning.

The feeling of being watched prickled through his body. He wondered if he should run, and, when he turned to go, something leathery batted him in the face.

"Aaaaagh!" Riley stumbled back and bumped into a tree. He leaned against the trunk, jerking his head back and forth, and up and down, as he sought out the thing that struck him.

A bone-chilling screech filled the air, freezing his blood. Panting, Riley pushed away from the tree and clambered up the hill.

The screeching grew nearer. Riley's throat constricted. He searched but couldn't find the source. Out of nowhere, something cut him across the cheek, knocking him over. Alarm raced through him. When he touched the cut, blood met his fingers. A claw, more than likely, had done that.

"But how?" he asked aloud. "What's attacking me?"

Everything quieted down for the moment, until leaves on the ground began to move— creating a trail no more than ten feet away—coming for him!

Riley scrambled back, too scared to do anything else. Why couldn't he see the creature in front of him?

There're no such thing as invisible creatures, he told himself. *But then again, Alan's a ghost . . .*

Whatever-it-was hissed. Riley squinted, trying to see the creature. If it even was a creature. Slowly, it appeared, shaping into a large bat, which took flight straight in the air right above Riley. It dive-bombed at him, but out of nowhere, a streak of crimson lightning struck it, sending it into the trees.

A man appeared. He lifted his hand and shouted, "Gaphladeen!" The crimson lightning sped further into the forest, and another bloodcurdling screech filled the air. It died down after a few seconds.

Breathing heavily, Riley stared in the direction of the where the lightning had sent the bat. After a minute or two, he turned towards the man who'd saved his life.

He wasn't exactly old, but he wasn't young either. He seemed sort of ageless. Green eyes peered down at Riley, penetrating and conscious of everything around him. The man's face was difficult to see in the evening dark, yet Riley could just make out a smile. Something about the man's smile looked kind.

What were his intentions, though?

The man approached and held his hand out. "Hello, Riley."

Riley gasped. "Whoa! How do you know my name?"

"I know more about you than you realize." The man's gentle expression never left his face. "You are the one with the star. The third child to have it. Thankfully, I got to you in time."

Could it be? Riley faltered briefly before taking the man's hand. "H-hi." Everything that'd taken place today made Riley think that, perhaps, this was all a dream? But no. It was all too real. As the man helped him up, Riley stammered, "A-are you . . . Dorobonn?"

Chapter Five

"Indeed," the fellow said, nodding. "I am Dorobonn."

This guy is Dorobonn. Alan must've told the truth! Riley looked to where the bat had been zapped. Was that lightning Dorobonn had used? It sure looked like lightning, but how did he do it?

Riley shook his head. "What did you do to the . . . gigantic bat that attacked me? And what do you mean by saying you got to me in time?"

"Not a bat, but a bloodpire. It is an evil creature that found its way into the Human World. No doubt, once it sensed you here, it came after you." Dorobonn glanced down the hill. "Come. There is much we have to talk about."

Riley hesitated as curiosity gnawed at him. *This is insane. Wait, he said "Human World" like . . . like there are other worlds out there.* The realization both thrilled and frightened him. He looked towards home. Light shined in the windows. Did his parents realize he was gone?

Sympathy wrapped around his heart. His parents didn't understand what was going on. *I didn't sneak out just for the fun of it. I couldn't have searched for answers if I hadn't have slipped out.*

Riley's legs refused to follow Dorobonn as he ambled through the forest. He knew next to nothing about this guy. What if he turned on Riley and used the lightning on him? Alan had said Dorobonn came here to help Riley, but what if Alan lied? Besides, Alan was a ghost. A *ghost.* Riley didn't believe in ghosts, but how else could he explain Alan? Part of him obstinately refused to think that this was happening at all. After a minute, Dorobonn stopped and peered over his shoulder at Riley. "Are you coming?"

"Oh!" Riley shook his head and scrambled down the slope. What if he couldn't trust this guy? He had no means of defending himself if Dorobonn turned on him.

"So, Dorobonn . . ." Riley began, "where did this star come from? Who are you? Why do I have it? What's going on? How did you do that lightning? I have this strange feeling in my eye, but I don't know how to describe it. I guess you could say it's a weird sort of tingly feeling." Riley paused, afraid he might be going too fast.

Dorobonn chuckled. "The feeling you get is nothing strange at all. It—the star—comes to you after you commit an act of bravery. Following every act of courage, it becomes more and more visible." He tilted his head. "The star originated with the People of the Symbol. The symbols matched each person's calling. There were all sorts of symbols. Each of them stood for something. The star for bravery, the cardinal's feather for compassion, the raindrop for a gentle spirit, the leaf for agility, and the flame for strength.

"I understand that John Alan O'Shea visited you. He is a good friend of mine. I trust he told you that you are the last one to have a star. Now, the previous star bearer was killed by a man named Iradocc, who is a demolic. He has made it his life's goal to kill all of the People of the Symbol. Legend says a star-bearer will defeat Iradocc, therefore he is determined to see you dead. Now that the Vile One is beginning his takeover, Iradocc will endeavor to kill us so as not to fail the Vile One in his reign. Iradocc is the most valued of the Vile One's soldiers. And to answer your last question, that lightning I used is magic."

"Wait." Dorobonn's words brought Riley to a halt. *The Vile One beginning his takeover? Fail the Vile One in his reign? Who's the Vile One? Who's Iradocc? Magic?* Something told him this was not, in fact, a dream—and if so, it unnerved him even more. He also recalled Alan having told him that Dorobonn was a Light Magician. That would explain the magic. "Who's the Vile One? And Iradocc is looking for *me*? I . . ." Riley trailed off. Facing a day with Bryan and Felix seemed far more preferable to being hunted down by a maniacal guy bent on destroying him. "How is this possible? Why do *I* have this star?"

"I already told you, child," Dorobonn sighed. "You have been marked with the star because you were chosen by Elomé. You have more courage than you realize. The star would not have come to just anyone. You have been marked for a reason, and yes, Iradocc is on the hunt for you. Luckily, he cannot come here, to the Human World, in-person. He is limited in that regard. The Vile One is his leader. A satanic ruler, at that."

Hmm. Riley needed time to think this through. "When I met Alan, he said I couldn't see him because I wasn't ready. I couldn't see the bat immediately, either. Why?"

"No human can see us unless they are ready—that is true. We are merely imagination and myth to them. You, however," Dorobonn said, poking Riley's chest with his forefinger, "are not blind to the magic that surrounds you. Many people miss it or have outgrown it. Not you. You have never lost it. You have shown valor in the face of adversity. Strength when needed. In this forest, there is a door nearby, as I am sure Alan told you. The Door of Tranien. Like us, it is only visible when you are ready to enter."

Riley's mind went back to his home. "Does anyone else in my family have a symbol?"

"No." Dorobonn shook his head. "Only you have the symbol."

"Alan said something about the world of Leíso. What is that place? And what is Zefa?"

"Leíso is the world on the other side of the door. Zefa is the village you must save."

"What if I'm ready now? Since I saw Alan and can see you, I must be," Riley reasoned.

With a chuckle, Dorobonn patted Riley's shoulder. "You will know when you are ready, child." An odd gleam in his eyes made Riley hesitate, as if he knew what Riley was thinking.

"You must defeat Iradocc in Zefa to achieve peace both there and in the Human World."

Talk about pressure! Before Riley knew it, they arrived to a double door near a clump of brush at the foot of a hill.

In spite of his doubts, exuberance filled Riley to his very core.

Dorobonn placed a hand on the door. "This is the gateway, so to speak, into Leíso. It is a magical world where creatures of all sorts dwell."

"Whoa. So, I have to defeat Iradocc? The guy you talked about earlier? How?" Riley glanced up the hill to his house. "How does any of this affect my world? You said I need to stop him in order to save . . . what'd you call it? The Human World?"

Dorobonn's smile faded. "Yes. You are a star-bearer. And if nothing is done to stop him the Dark Magic Iradocc wields will spread into the Human World."

Riley's throat went dry. "You mean he can get into the Human World? But I thought you said—"

"No. He can't, but he has ways to get around that."

The air felt too warm. Perspiration beaded Riley's neck. "Why can't you beat him, Dorobonn?" Riley asked, pinching the front of his shirt with his forefinger and thumb.

"I told you, child. Only one with a star can. It is a prophesy that must be fulfilled. You are the one with the star who must defeat him."

Uncertainty and apprehension made Riley's heart sink. "Sooo . . . what if I don't ever feel ready?"

Dorobonn didn't answer for a while. He finally looked at Riley with sorrowful eyes and said, "Then everyone will die. In the world beyond the door, and in your world."

"Umm." Riley swallowed hard as he gazed at the door. Could he go through with it and battle someone who wanted him dead? He didn't doubt Iradocc practiced magic. Fighting Bryan would definitely be more of a cake walk compared to this.

Dorobonn's hand touched his arm. "I trust you and your decision. I must leave now. I will see you again. Soon." He eyed Riley's face and nodded. "You might also want to see to that cut on your cheek." Riley reached up and touched it, wincing, having forgotten it was there.

As Dorobonn turned to leave, Riley still needed to ask a question burning inside of him. "Dorobonn, when I come into Leíso, how will I know where to meet you?"

Dorobonn smiled kindly. "Do not focus on that now. Getting into Leíso is your first challenge." And with nothing but an odd blur, the door opened, and Dorobonn disappeared through it.

Riley watched in amazement. Soon after Dorobonn left, Riley grabbed the knob and pulled. It wouldn't budge.

Weird. He shrugged and headed back to his house, using moonlight to guide him. He trekked up the hill and, when he reached his house and started to climb up the tree, a shriek sounded in the distance.

The bloodpire? But it had been killed, right? *Is there a second one?*

He risked a glimpse over his shoulder but saw nothing. *I need to get to bed!* He pulled himself up and opened the window.

A waft of cold air hit the wound on his cheek. Riley hesitated for a moment and then scooted through the window. Grabbing the window to shut it, he detected someone nearby and lowered his gaze.

Standing beneath the window, a dark-haired man with a razor-sharp fang and evil blue eyes stared up at Riley. The man grinned and his fang glinted like a knife in the moonlight.

"You cannot hide from us. I look forward to making your acquaintance."

"Who-who are you?" Riley stammered. The malice emanating from this man was strong.

"You'll find out soon enough." He then glowered. "Stay out of my business. Otherwise, your punishment will be far worse than the wound I gave you."

Goosebumps rose across Riley's arms. With a grunt, he slammed the window shut, locked it, and pulled the curtains together. Throat dry, Riley forced a swallow. Who was that man and what did he mean by telling Riley to stay out of his business? Not to mention, the man said he looked forward to making Riley's acquaintance. You would not say that to someone and then warn them to leave you alone. Groaning, Riley rubbed his face with his hands, grimacing at the pain from his wound.

After he washed the concealer from his eye, he cleaned his

cut, which wasn't as deep as he'd feared, and then texted Caroline.

- *"Hey, would ya mind meeting me in the forest behind my house tomorrow morning? 6 a.m., before class?*
- *Sure!"*

After putting on his pajamas, Riley turned to the window. Taking a deep breath, he moved the curtain a smidge and peeked out. The man had left. Hopefully. Keeping an eye on the window, Riley laid down in his bed. *I guess I'll find out tomorrow if I can see Leíso.*

* * *

Early the next morning, Riley jumped out of bed and crept to his door. He hoped his parents weren't awake. Tiptoeing into the hallway, he halted at the sound of his parents' voices. Creeping lightly halfway down the stairs, he caught sight of them standing in the kitchen.

"Until we get this star matter settled, how can Riley explain it to his principal. He has to let Mr. Davis know about Bryan," his mother said with a sigh.

"Yes. I agree. Perhaps he should see a counselor," his father suggested, though it sounded more like a question than a statement. "Riley wouldn't get a tattoo until he was old enough. We'll have a talk with him when he gets home from school."

Riley blinked. So much his parents didn't know. Guilt weighed on him heavily. He couldn't mention the bloodpire, they'd never believe him.

He backed slowly into his room. There was only one thing to do now. *I've gotta get out of here and find out how to open that door!* He got dressed, and opened the window. The dark-haired man was nowhere to be seen. Maybe he was gone for good? Riley climbed onto the tree. His belly growled, but he couldn't think about breakfast. Not now. When he reached the ground, a text arrived from Caroline.

- *Hey! I'm on the way! Gimme a moment.*

She texted him again about fifteen minutes later, saying she was in his driveway. When he saw her at the edge of the forest, he waved. She climbed down the slope and then stared at Riley's star.

He glanced to the side, self-conscious and cleared his throat.

"What's going on?" Caroline asked. Gasping, she squinted at his cheek. "Where'd you get that cut?"

Riley winced at the worry in her voice. "I . . . I got it from climbing the tree outside my room yesterday." The lie slipped out so easily, Riley pursed his lips. Caroline didn't even seem to believe him, however. He needed to change the subject, fast! "I need to show you something."

"Did you tell your parents about the star?" Caroline asked.

Riley faltered. "Err . . . yeah. They . . . they thought it was a tattoo. They want me to get rid of it."

"Can you?"

"Not—not really."

"What do you mean?"

"Follow me, and I'll explain everything."

Overhead, darkening clouds threatened a storm, bringing with it, the scent of rain. As they entered the forest, cold air surrounded them. No breeze. No sounds. Even Caroline stayed silent. He glanced over his shoulder, but she eyed the ground. He didn't know what to make of that.

The door appeared not far ahead. Riley pointed at it. "There it is!" He ran, motioning to Caroline. "C'mon!"

Her expression turned from impassive to confused.

She can see it, right?

"Okay. So, a guy named Dorobonn visited me recently. He said that I am a part of a line of people who had symbols a long time ago. Symbols like my star. Two of them did have a star before me, but . . . they died." Riley scratched the back of his neck. "Anyway. In Leíso, which is behind this door, a demolic named Iradocc is wanting to kill me. He uses Dark Magic, as he is a Dark Magician. So, Dorobonn said that I have to learn magic in order to battle Iradocc." Saying these things aloud, Riley tried not to grimace at how weird they might've sounded. "Now, I'm going to show you exactly what I mean about this door, which is called the Door of Tranien. Watch." Riley grabbed the knob and pulled.

It didn't do anything.

"Wha—?" The door remained fixed. *But why? I'm ready!* He pulled again, but nothing happened. "Nooo."

The wind picked up, bringing a few droplets of rain with it.

"Riley, the rain's coming. I need to get going."

"The door will open. Trust me!" He yanked it again.

"It doesn't seem the . . . 'Door of Tranien' wants to open."

Something in her tone threw him off. She'd said the word "door" like it didn't exist.

Riley turned to her and then eyed the door. "You can see it, can't you?"

Her silence was like a wall between them. "No," she said, seemingly struggling between telling him the truth and being sympathetic. The sympathy annoyed Riley. It made him feel like a child. "I only see a tree."

She couldn't see the door?

Dorobonn had said something about others not seeing it.

Was her confusion from earlier any mystery now? Riley grunted and let go of the knob. It was no use explaining the situation when the evidence wouldn't present itself.

"Okay. I'm sorry. I . . ." He stared at the ground. Caroline didn't say anything. She opened her mouth to speak, but then closed it. Riley avoided eye contact with her as they headed back up the hill. *If she can't see it, then why would anyone else? She probably thinks I'm nuts now. Fantastic.* The thought both aggravated and upset Riley. A bloodpire's screech sounded somewhere off in the distance. Riley wavered and looked over his shoulder. There it was again! Thankfully, nowhere near them. Chills crawled up his spine, but when he glanced at Caroline, she didn't seem to notice.

She can't hear it. Maybe no one else can.

Chapter Six

After Caroline left, Riley followed her to the edge of the forest and leaned against a tree. The pouring rain dampened both his body and spirit. Caroline hadn't bothered staying. He'd seen the fear in her eyes. She didn't believe him. *What I wouldn't give to have people believe this star is not a tattoo and that the door is real.*

He wished the rain might be able to wash away the chaos raging within his heart, somehow. "Ugh. I can't stay out here forever," he mumbled.

He checked his phone. *Oh no.* He had three missed calls from his dad. How had he not heard those? Riley gazed up at his house in the distance, willing his eyes to stay open as the rain pelted him.

A light turned on in his room, like a flame to lead him home. The figure of his mom stood in the window. Riley's heart sank. The accusations of his parents—and their misunderstanding—rang in his ears. Riley knew, however, that they were simply worried about him. He recalled the concern in his dad's voice as they'd discussed how they should help Riley.

Help. They wanted to help. That realization gave Riley a better understanding of his parents' position on the matter.

Right now, he needed to know why the door hadn't budged. *Caroline couldn't see it, but I could. It's weird, though. It wouldn't open. So, there seems to be some 50/50 chance that it will or won't open depending on who's around.* Trying to figure out all the possibilities just served to confuse him more.

His mom moved away from the window and the room went dark again—the guiding flame snuffed out.

Rivulets of rainwater and mud streamed down the hill. Riley stood up, soaked to the bone. Riley turned and made his way back through the trees. Eyeing the door, he reached for the knob . . .

I wonder.

"I suppose you weren't ready earlier?"

The voice startled Riley, who turned to the owner and forgot the knob.

"Alan!" Riley had never been so happy to see anyone—or anything, that is.

The ghost ambled to the door and stuck his hands in his oversized robe pockets. "I witnessed the entire situation. Your friend seemed skeptical from the start."

Riley bristled. "Then why didn't you show up? That could've probably helped."

The corner of Alan's mouth notched up. "No, lad. She wouldn't 'ave been able to see me anyways. *You* would 'ave, obviously, but not your friend."

Riley lowered his head and sighed. "Sorry. I didn't mean to snap. I'm just—it's . . . it's super frustrating to have to deal with this by myself. No one can see what I see, like the door. At least not Caroline, the only person that I tried to show. My parents don't know what to think about my star. They think it's a tattoo."

Alan glanced down and rubbed his lips together, as though deciding whether or not to speak what was on his mind. "I certainly understand your irritation about all of this. You cannot force anyone else to see the door, as you know, but with enough persuasion, your friend will be able to see it. 'owever . . ." Alan stepped closer. "I do not know if you've realized this, Riley, but your star is fading."

What? Riley turned his phone's camera on. He gasped. The star *was* fading! "How?"

"You are not as confident as you were before. Once you are no longer sure of yourself, the star will disappear. At that moment, you may never receive it back."

Never receive it back? Why? Riley raised his head, prepared to ask Alan what he meant, but the ghost had disappeared.

"Who were you talking to?"

Caroline's voice nearly made him jump.

"I . . ." What could he say? If he said a ghost, who knew how she'd react? Therefore, he slowly closed his mouth and looked away. No use telling her if she wouldn't believe him.

Caroline lowered her eyes. "I . . . I'll admit, I am curious about everything you told me."

Riley turned to the door as Dorobonn's words echoed in his mind. If he didn't fight Dark Magic then both the Human World and Leíso would be obliterated. Whether or not Caroline believed him, he needed to do this. It would be best, however, not to go at it alone. Summoning resolve, Riley gestured to the door. He would make this work! "Alan visited me. He's a ghost. The one who originally told me about the star." Riley took a step towards her. "Now, I know what you're gonna say, that it's all in my head. But, you have to trust me, Caroline. This tree you're seeing is actually a *door*."

Caroline cocked a brow. "Riley. I don't know."

Determined, Riley motioned to his face. "You see my star, right?"

She nodded.

"That's only the beginning. Believe me when I say the door is real, and it leads to a different world called Leíso. You must trust me."

Caroline closed her eyes and sighed, clearly struggling.

The air went still, as though waiting for her to speak.

"Okay," she said, "to be honest, I do want to believe you. I . . . I think it would be amazing to see other worlds. I don't know how that would be possible, but I would love to do that—see other worlds, that is."

Riley heard the reservation in Caroline's words and almost told her she didn't have to come when her eyes grew round and she touched her fingers to her mouth.

"What is it?" Riley asked cautiously.

She pointed straight at the door, dumbfounded. "It's–it's there. Riley, it—the door! It's there!"

Riley stood there in dismay. Could Caroline finally see the door?

"You're not just saying that, are you?" He wanted to make sure before raising his hopes too high.

Caroline didn't answer. She reached out and touched the door and softly ran her hand over the iron knob.

Riley's excitement spiked. *She can see it! Yes!* He could've jumped for joy, but he simply smiled, encouraged by her words.

"We're ready." He then paused. "D-do you want to go, too?"

Caroline nodded, staring ahead determinedly (if a tad reluctant). "You don't have to go at it alone."

Riley, grateful for her willingness to come with him, reached for the knob and slowly pulled open the door.

Chapter Seven

Leíso. The world beyond their own, and beyond anything he could ever imagine. Riley's heart somersaulted. He couldn't believe it! The sun hung on the west side of the horizon, hinting at evening. The light glimmered between tree branches bearing leaves of such a deep green hue that they mesmerized Riley. Being later in the day, a serene warmth hung in the air. These trees were different from the ones at home. Lush moss grew on their trunks, encircling their bases. The air smelt fresh and sweet, as the landscape was dotted with colorful flowers. A little stream gurgled only a few feet away. Mossy stones nestled here and there throughout the forest floor. Riley glanced behind him, amazed at the stark contrast in weather between his world and this world. Sun shone in Leíso, giving the forest an emerald glow, whereas, in the forest they left behind, a deluge poured on a cold, dreary day.

"This is so amazing," Caroline breathed. "If I wasn't actually here myself, I'd think this was all just a dream. Hold on . . ." she wavered. "How do we know for sure that it is, in fact, real?"

Riley furrowed his brows. "What do you mean?"

Caroline motioned to the forest. "The stream could've come from a picture in a fairy tale book. That is . . . I mean . . . how do we know it's all real and not our . . ."

She didn't finish the sentence, but Riley assumed she was going to say "imagination."

He touched her shoulder. "Don't you think it'd be strange for the two of us to both the imagining the same thing at the same time?"

As they crept through the forest, Riley wondered if anyone lived here.

There was a cheeriness in the air that Riley had only experienced on sunnier days at home. The birds seemed normal. Their happy chirps brought light to Riley's heart. One bird, in particular, a greenish-blue one with silky feathers—about the size of his palm—sang with a sound similar to that of chimes. Wind chimes, to be exact. So peaceful and sweet. There was something else, too.

Belonging. Could it be that he'd always longed for this place but could never exactly pinpoint the feeling?

"Riley! It looks like a shelter." Caroline pointed a hovel of sorts in the distance. It appeared to sit at the edge of the forest.

Riley grabbed Caroline's hand and dashed forward, careful of stones and tree roots. He didn't slow down until they broke through the trees at the edge of a village.

Small huts, stone hovels, and clay houses dotted the area. People and unusual elven-sorts were strolling about the market stalls while children played. To his right, a white and gray stone castle towered above the village. Its multicolored flags waved in the wind.

Many of the villagers regarded the two travelers in confusion. Had they never seen people before?

They look human, too.

A mother with her children shuffled by. If one of them stole so much as a glimpse of Riley or Caroline, she scolded, "No! We do not associate with *them*."

Huh?

An elderly couple didn't even bother looking up. When the wife turned her head the slightest bit, she immediately jerked away. Most of the reactions they received from the villagers were either hostile or wary.

Humans—at least, they looked like humans—populated the village, even though many had very pale skin. Others had darker skin the color of reddish-brown Autumn leaves. There were also creatures with pointy ears. Riley recalled what he'd read about elves in his fantasy books but couldn't quite place these. Their eyes appeared human, and all of them had a slightly greenish and silver complexion, but the tips of their ears reached their crowns—far longer than the elves in the books he'd read. They weren't even the most unusual! A handful of creatures looked similar to rodents, with rounded, fuzz-lined ears, tiny sharp teeth, and tails poking out of their backsides.

"Oi!"

Riley turned to five guards marching towards them. *Uh oh.*

He shielded Caroline with his arm.

The leader halted and sized Riley up. His oily black hair parted in the middle, and his dark brown eyes pierced Riley's.

"You there, boy! I am Edilie. The guard of the Royal Castle of Zefa. I keep intruders out of the village." The guard leveled his spear at Riley's chest. "What do you think you're doing here?"

Riley sidled away from the tip, words slipping off his tongue. "Err . . . my friend and I just came to this village by mistake." He fought to keep from looking away after telling that lie. "We don't mean any trouble, but we came through a door."

The guard scowled. "A door? What kind of door?"

Riley swept a hand to the forest. "A door somewhere back there. We're from the Human World."

Edilie poked him in the chest with his spear. "Human World? You're the Human Worlders I heard about!"

Already?

The guard paused. "Why do you have that accursed star on your eye?"

"Because . . . because it just, well, appeared one day." Riley peered down at the weapon, hoping the guard wouldn't stab him without warning. Besides, he didn't trust this guard enough to explain just why he and Caroline were here.

"Well, then. I will order you, right now, to leave!" Edilie snarled.

Riley lifted his hands. "Hey, look. There's someone I need to find. I'll leave after I see him."

The guard didn't move the spear. He kept it at only inches from Riley's chest. Riley and Caroline exchanged glances.

"No, you will leave at once!"

Riley peered at the curious villagers crowding around, but no one butted in. Most of all, he feared for Caroline's safety. While he didn't doubt she could take care of herself, he had no desire for her to have to prove that right here and now.

"If you don't leave," the guard hissed, "I will kill you. Human Worlders invade our world and take over however they please. We will not stand for it."

"Wait, there've been other Human Worlders besides us? Really?" Riley said. He couldn't remember either Dorobonn or Alan mentioning that.

"Yes," the guard spat, "and we shall not put up with any more of you scoundrels."

Scoundrels?

"If you do not leave right now, you will die!" the guard snapped, leveling his arm back, as if to act upon his word.

"Edilie!" a voice called out from the crowd. "That is enough!"

The villagers parted the way for a well-dressed man with brown, neatly combed hair, a dark green suit and breeches. A scabbard hung from his belt and his gaze exuded authority. The outfit suggested a higher position than Edilie's.

"It is not your decision whether or not people are allowed into Zefa, but mine. Allow this young man and his friend entrance. They will meet Princess Lunaira. Not all Human Worlders are evil. You know that."

Several moments passed before Edilie acquiesced.

"Very well." He threw Riley a murderous glance, then backed off for the other fellow.

"Welcome, friends," the other man said. "My name is Matthew. I am the first-in-command and steward of Princess Lunaira. You must forgive Edilie. We have had unwanted visits by those hailing from the Human World. In any case, I shall have you escorted to her majesty's castle immediately. I am certain she will wish to make your acquaintance." His gray eyes rested on Riley for a moment before he gestured for them to follow.

The castle gleamed in the sunlight. A couple of the guards opened the large doors to reveal a hallway leading to a door on the other side. Possibly the throne room. Unfortunately, Edilie was one of the guards who'd opened a door. Riley stared ahead, trying to avoid eye contact, but the guard caught him—none too gently—by the shoulder, and hissed in his ear, "If you dare do anything to disrupt our lives here with that symbol of yours, you won't live to regret it."

Not knowing what to say, Riley pried his shoulder from

Edilie's grasp and sped up his steps to catch up to Matthew and Caroline.

"Your Highness!" Matthew announced.

A young woman, Riley assumed to be the princess, stood in the doorway of the room at the end of the hall with her hands clasped in front of her. Her black hair reached down to her waist. A silky green dress hung from her shoulders, and swept the floor as she moved. Her mysterious, deep blue eyes pierced Riley with the intensity of arrows. He couldn't tell if what he saw in her gaze was mistrust or something else.

"Good afternoon, friends." A kind smile reached her eyes. "I am Princess Lunaira of Zefa." Matthew bowed and then gestured to Riley and Caroline. "Your Highness, these two travelers hail from the Human World." He stepped aside for the princess.

"Hello, your Highness." Riley bowed, and Caroline curtsied. "My name is Riley. This is my friend, Caroline. We came through a door in the forest." He waved a hand in the direction of the village. "And . . . well, we just ended up here, and we're curious to know more about this place."

Princess Lunaira gently bobbed her head. "And we are glad to have you. You are welcomed to stay here for as long as you like. We do not receive many visitors from the Human World. Unfortunately, quite a few who have come did not do so with good intentions. However, there have been pleasant ones, and I believe that you are of that sort, so this is a rare treat indeed! Do come in. There is much I wish to know."

How would she know we have good intentions? Riley didn't bother voicing this question aloud. No need to give the princess any reason to be suspicious. Inside, the castle was breathtaking. Tapestries hung on the walls, featuring ancient kings and queens and great battles. Some sort of language was printed on these tapestries, which piqued Riley's curiosity. Stained glass windows threw rainbow lighting onto the brown and tan patterned carpet. Three doors lined the walls on their left. Two were shut, but one was partially open, revealing a room full of books.

Hmm. What kind of books do Zefans read?

"We were not expecting visitors, but if you are hungry, the kitchen staff could bring out some food for you. After all, it is almost dinnertime." Princess Lunaira stood beside an open door that led to flight of stairs leading down. Riley caught a faint orange glow from the stairway and heard the clatter of silverware. The savory scent of bread and grilled meat wafted up.

Caroline nodded vigorously before he could say anything. "Yes, please!" she exclaimed. "Thank you very much."

At that moment, Riley's stomach growled. He'd not eaten anything since yesterday morning at his parents', and he was starving. The small portion of spaghetti he had eaten last night didn't count.

Once everyone was seated in the dining hall, the servers brought in the food. Five candles lined the beautiful marble dining table, casting an almost eerie glow on the surface. The food looked exquisite and smelled amazing. In the middle of the table, two loaves of bread sat on porcelain platters with bowls of butter, and another platter held thick slices of ham. Sitting alongside the ham, a bowl of garlic mashed potatoes. Glass goblets of water were placed before Lunaira, Matthew, Riley, and Caroline.

As they ate, Riley felt someone's gaze on him. Edilie was nowhere to be seen. Lunaira wasn't looking at him either. He peeked to the side and found Matthew eyeing him—or, was he staring at Riley's star? Either way, Riley acted as if he didn't notice, even though the opposite was true.

"I am quite curious about you two. What can you tell me about this door you found?" Lunaira asked.

"Umm. We just found it in the forest and went through it." Riley didn't think it necessary to explain the entire situation to Lunaira. He didn't know how she'd respond or if he could fully trust her. "I don't know if the door has always been there, but when we discovered it, we decided to see what was on the other side."

He also didn't expect to stay for too long. He needed to find Dorobonn and figure out how to fight Iradocc. He had no idea what Caroline was thinking. She remained silent. Did she want to stay?

"We are glad to have you. I am not sure if you have been properly informed about this world, but it is called Leíso. I assume you've already learned the name of the village." With that, Lunaira swept a wry glance at Edilie. "Zefa resides within the Kingdom of Althia. It was named by one of our beloved queens from years past, the wife of the king who came from the Human World. King Phillip." Lunaira turned to Caroline. "I am happy to have another girl here to talk to. My sister lives in another kingdom, far away. The company will be nice."

"I appreciate it." Caroline smiled, but Riley believed it was simply to be polite. "I would love to hang out."

Despite the slightly awkward atmosphere, Riley enjoyed everything on his plate. The bread was so soft, and the butter melted on it so nicely. Caroline ate her food more slowly, and Riley didn't think it was because she wanted to savor it. Guilt pricked him in the stomach, stalling his appetite. They wouldn't stay longer than necessary. After all, if he needed to battle a demolic (whatever that entailed), he'd want to get it over with as soon as possible!

After their meal, Riley excused himself to explore the castle. He asked Lunaira if he could check out the library.

Although she didn't say anything, she dipped her head, yes. Odd. She'd spoken to him earlier. What was the deal? Caroline started to get up as well, but Lunaira stopped her, wishing to speak with her a bit longer. Caroline obliged, if a bit hesitantly.

On the way to the library, Riley wondered if Caroline was going to come with him or do something herself. Lunaira didn't seem interested in conversing with him. In fact, she appeared a little unsure whenever she looked at Riley during dinner. *Hm.* Shrugging it off, he searched the hall for the library while hoping to avoid Edilie. He remembered seeing the door to the library near the castle's entrance. To his relief, the guard was nowhere in sight.

"Edilie, my friend, why are you vengeful towards the boy?"

The voice came from around a corner to his right. Riley slowed down then put his back to the wall and listened. Somehow, he knew that, whoever spoke, was referring to him.

"Is it that obvious?" a grouchy voice muttered in return. Riley assumed it belonged to Edilie.

"Please, my friend, you've been stewing for the past forty–five minutes."

Edilie growled. "How can you know what I'm angry about? I haven't said anything."

A pause followed. "You don't have to. I'm aware of your . . . history." The fellow guard didn't expound on his comment.

"How would you know?" Edilie's surprised tone didn't faze the other guard one bit, considering his calm response,

"It's no mystery, my friend." Footsteps drew close and Riley pressed himself to the wall. A column hid him from view —if the guards continued straight ahead. If they turned the corner, he'd likely be discovered. The situation with him running away and hiding from Bryan at school suddenly flashed through his mind. Riley closed his eyes, working to shut out the memory and keep himself from panicking. Thank goodness, the guards walked on, heedless of the boy spying on them. Waiting until they were out of sight, Riley found himself at a dead end.

Don't tell me I have to go the same way as those guys. Groaning, Riley rolled his eyes at the irony and, as quiet as a mouse, snuck down the hall, praying they wouldn't pop out from around the corner. Particularly Edilie. Fortunately for him, they'd gone somewhere else. Unfortunately, the castle was more of a maze than he'd expected. Where was he going? It didn't seem *this* complicated earlier. Then again, he'd only come through here once and had followed those who lived here. Ah! There. Just as he touched the knob, the door cracked open, as if beckoning him to enter. Stomach twisting, Riley pulled his hand back. Had it opened by itself or by a draft in the castle? He hoped the latter possibility. Perhaps a ghost? Alan was a ghost, so who was to say more ghosts didn't exist in this world? The idea didn't bring him comfort.

Unwilling to be scared off, however, Riley carefully took hold of the knob and pushed. Candelabras lit the room, casting light on to the various-colored stones, giving it an interesting silver and golden-like appearance. A mirror hung from the wall, opposite the window facing outside. The sweet and musty scent of old books made him sigh, blissful. The shelves reached the ceiling, which was probably about fifteen feet high. Golden letters stood out on the spines, and he ran his fingers over them, indulging in the leathery and rough textures. One book stood out to him, as it hung an inch or so over the shelf. He gently pulled it out.

The book was larger than he realized and very thick. The title read, *Nölv ec doln Clareisthia.* He set it down on the one wooden table in the room and flipped through the pages.

So many pages!

Sheesh! What's this thing about? On the bottom of the very first page, he found words written in script. He read them aloud, "For those of the Human World, speak 'Delnví'."

When he turned the page, everything translated into English! He glanced at the cover—"The Book of Interpretation." *Interpretation?*

"Whoa!" He turned another page. Again, the words melded into English from its previous text. The fourth page said, "The Words of the Ancient Light Magic," followed by unusual words in no language he recognized. Maybe the English translation hadn't gotten to them yet?

Words of the Ancient Light Magic?

"Gaaaphhladeeen." Riley sounded out the first word, letting it roll off his tongue.

A fluttery feeling tickled his chest. He glanced down, not seeing anything.

"Pal-palst-palstona." The tickle grew into a flame. Disconcerted, he clapped his hand to his chest. *That was weird!*

This time, he whispered, "Il-il-ilíeeeeanda?" His star buzzed, for a moment, then stopped. Strange. Soon after, his hands, too, buzzed and then normal again.

Magic? Light Magic?

There!—a page with the title, "The People of the Symbol." Dorobonn and Alan had talked about these people!

"The People of the Symbol were a peaceful civilization of farmers, merchants, travelers, blacksmiths, magic-traders, and more," he read. "Each person had a symbol correlating with their calling. For instance, the cardinal's feather represented peace and healing. Many individuals with a cardinal's feather were arbitrators, who usually served the royals. A leaf symbolized agility. These people would become messengers or farmers. There were various other symbols, but the most unique was a star. Only two people have had the star. The first was killed in battle. The second was a child slaughtered by Iradocc."

"Hello, Riley."

Riley jumped back from the book. For a split second, he thought Edilie had said his name. Then again, the guard wouldn't have been *that* polite. Not to mention, the voice was decidedly more feminine. He turned towards Princess Lunaira, who stood in the doorway with a friendly smile. Strange.

"Caroline is looking at the room my staff provided for her. Ah! I see you are reading *The Book of Interpretation*—otherwise known as the magic book. I have not read much of it," she said, "only what was required for my history lessons as a child."

She chuckled and sat in the chair across from him. "When I saw your star when you arrived it amazed me. I had not expected to see the line of the star continue in my lifetime. This is truly incredible."

Riley gave her a half-hearted smile then pointed at the page with a frown. "I learned recently that there were two others with the star. Is there anything in here that says when or how the first person died? I wasn't told."

The princess leaned over and read the passage. Upon finishing, Lunaira sighed. "There is a prophecy about it in the back of the book. Three people throughout history will have a star. If neither the first nor the second can defeat Iradocc—Iradocc is a demolic from Haedian—" she explained, "the third person must. Otherwise, all is lost."

Almost exactly what Dorobonn and Alan had said.

He was about to repeat his question, as Lunaira hadn't answered it. She continued before he said anything. "I do not know why the first one's death is not explained in this book. I learned it from an old professor of mine years ago who's passed on. If I remember my history lessons correctly, he—the first person with the star—died as a young man. How old are you, Riley?"

"Sixteen."

"He was eighteen when he died. He tried to challenge the warlord of the kingdom of Sorona—which is now the kingdom of Arlock. The warlord was a follower of Iradocc. Then about 200 years later, the second one with the star came along. Sadly, as you've read, the child was killed at an early age."

Both died young. Riley took a deep breath, attempting to keep the queasiness at bay.

"So. I'm the third one. And the two before me died at young ages." He forced himself to focus on a different matter, such as the other symbols.

Before Lunaira could say more on the subject, he flipped back to the fourth page. "What are these magic words?" He pointed to one and read it aloud. "Gaphladeen."

"That is what the magic-traders of the People of the Symbol learned. Not all of them could do magic, only the ones who were called. The prophecy didn't state whether or not the one with the star—the one who would defeat Iradocc—had magic. I don't doubt that it's possible." Her gaze towards Riley revealed her thoughts. Maybe he could do magic.

"Iradocc has already started ravaging far-off kingdoms by the Vile One's orders." Her tone sobered. "Some have begun to follow him, and it has become more difficult to tell friend from foe. As a result, those who were once united are being torn apart. I can only pray this does not continue for much longer. Otherwise, the kingdom itself is in jeopardy."

The princess stood up and headed for the door. "However, I do not wish for you to risk your life without knowing what you're getting into, Riley. If you feel you must go back home, you can." How interesting that she acted nice to him now, but at the dinner table, she'd barely said anything to him. Oh well.

The book in front of Riley surely had answers. The question was, could he figure it all out before Iradocc attacked?

Chapter Eight

Riley studied the book for about an hour or so after Lunaira left. He flexed his fingers and imagined some sort of lightning, like Dorobonn's, shooting out of his hand. Inspecting his palm, Riley whispered, "Gaphladeen." A static current traveled down his arm and into his palm, similar to the feeling he got when his hand fell asleep . . . tiny pinpricks.

A crimson spark popped in his palm. *Whoa—!* He closed his hand, opened it, and moved his fingers around. He clenched and unclenched it once more. The spark looked similar to the red electricity Dorobonn had used. Moonlight seeped through the library's window. One of the servants knocked and offered Riley a candle by which to read the book and gave him directions to his room.

The candle's flame illuminated the pages. Riley read every magic word carefully. He didn't know what each did, but he liked how Lunaira suspected he might be capable of magic. Had both people with the star possessed the ability to do magic? Before Riley closed the book, he flipped to a random page, just out of curiosity. On one side of a page, it was blank. *Huh?* Why would it be empty? No, wait. At the bottom of the page before it, Riley spotted the statement: "Only one with a pure heart, who has gone through many trials, may read what comes next."

Who would that be? Too exhausted for speculation, Riley yawned, closed the book, and put it back on the shelf. He wasn't sure what time it was as he headed to his room.

"Riley!" Caroline stood in the doorway of her room. Arms crossed, she crept up to him. "About earlier . . . I—whenever we can leave, I'd like to. I don't mind hanging out with Lunaira, but for some reason, I just don't feel really comfortable here. In this world."

Riley nodded, a tad disappointed. He felt fine in this world. "Okay. We'll figure out a plan. I still need to know more about Dark Magic, and I need to search for Dorobonn."

Caroline gave him a small smile and started back for her room. "You know, if you want to stay here, you can. I'm, personally, just ready to go home." She said nothing more, and neither did Riley. He wished Caroline wasn't in such a hurry to leave.

Eyelids heavy, Riley meandered to his room and flopped onto the bed, falling asleep as soon as he closed his eyes.

Hearing a disturbing chuckle in his ear, his eyes shot open. Darkness surrounded him. No moonlight filtered through the curtains.

The chuckle faded. A tiny dot of light fluttered past him. Riley watched as it floated above his head and then vanished. The blanket and sheets were no longer there. He felt the ground, which was rough, like dirt and rock.

What's going on? Where am I?

He couldn't hear a thing. The silence was deafening.

"I know you are here," a malicious voice drawled. "You

cannot hide from me. Try as you might, you will not escape, and I *shall* kill you."

None of the magic words Riley had read came to mind. He stood on trembling legs, willing himself to recall at least one.

Another flicker of light floated past him. Or perhaps it was the same one. He reached out to touch it. As soon as his fingers made contact, the light erupted into flame.

Riley yelped and fell back with a grunt. He scrambled away as the flame increased in size and became a giant, terrifying, manlike form with evil, smoldering blue eyes. The figure's armor, the color of blood, gleamed in the firelight. Disheveled platinum blonde hair shadowed his face. He watched Riley with such intensity, it made the boy shudder.

The man drew a fiery, curved sword from his scabbard, with sharp iron tips at the ends reaching for each other. He pointed it straight at Riley.

Too horrified to move, Riley stared at the flaming sword as the man leveled it back.

"I, Iradocc, will not be defeated by a mere child! I destroyed the People of the Symbol! None shall be left alive to overpower me!" the man—Iradocc—roared and stabbed his blade for Riley's heart.

Riley screamed and jolted awake. He clasped a hand to his chest. No blood. It'd been a bad dream. No, a nightmare. He swallowed hard, looking furtively about the room. No sign of a monster-man carrying a flaming sword and wearing red armor. Moonlight poured through the slit in the curtains on the opposite side of the room. He breathed heavily and leaned back against the pillow as his heart filled the silence with its frantic beating. Sweat drenched his back and face.

A nightmare.

Iradocc.

Riley closed his eyes and rubbed them hard with his fists.

Such a realistic nightmare! A fleeting pain seared his chest, over his heart. Alarmed, Riley lifted his shirt and looked down. To his horror, he noticed, what looked like, a small burn—black and raw. In the dim moonlight, he could see that its outline looked precisely like that of the curved sword Iradocc had been wielding.

It hadn't been just all in his head.

Riley sat on the edge of the bed and replayed the nightmare. Iradocc threatened to kill him and would stop at nothing to do so.

I need to find Dorobonn. Today.

Tentatively, he laid back down and stared at the ceiling, too nervous to close his eyes. Eventually, he drifted off into a restless sleep. Once morning arrived, he jumped out of bed and ran to the mirror at the opposite wall. *Is my star still visible?* The early dawn's light, though not terribly bright, gave him enough to see that the star was still there. *Whew!* Even though he'd been afraid in his dream, he hadn't lost the star.

In the hallway, Matthew greeted him. Like Lunaira, the steward acted normal as he talked to Riley. "Would you care for breakfast? Princess Lunaira had the kitchen staff prepare a meal this morning."

Riley glanced at the castle door, but when the wonderful scents of sweet bread and fruit wafted towards him, his hunger overcame his desire to find Dorobonn.

Throughout breakfast, Riley's mind wandered to the nightmare. He wouldn't tell Lunaira or Caroline about it and risk frightening them. Hopefully, Dorobonn would have answers.

"You are free to roam the village as you like," Lunaira said. "Do not hesitate to ask questions, and please stay as long as you wish. But whenever you are ready to leave and return to your world, you may."

This was the second time she'd told them this, but Riley

couldn't tell if she wanted them to leave or if she was simply letting them know they had a choice. The second option didn't offer much comfort. Riley sure hoped they had a choice! It seemed Caroline thought the same way. Her brows furrowed, but she made no comment.

Caroline glanced at Riley and he could tell she was growing a little uncomfortable. What did she and Lunaira talk about, anyway? Did their conversations make her uneasy? But she said she didn't mind hanging out with Lunaira. Riley turned to the princess. "Your highness?"

"Please, call me Lunaira."

"Lunaira. Do you know where Dorobonn lives? He's a magician."

"Hmm. I have heard of him, but I don't know where he lives. Why?" Her tone sounded a bit defensive.

"He . . ." Riley hesitated. How much should he share with her? "I met him in the Human World, and I need to see him again."

In his periphery, Caroline gave him a funny look.

"He is here in Zefa," Lunaira said. "That much I know. But I could not tell you where he lives."

Riley nodded his thanks, but wondered why Lunaira acted almost suspicious with him one moment and then friendly the next. After they finished eating, Lunaira took Caroline with her into her room. Riley needed to ask Caroline, at some point, if she felt uneasy with Lunaira. Even if it was none of his business, he wanted to make sure his friend wasn't upset by something the princess might've said to her. Then again, Caroline knew how to refuse company when need-be. No doubt she was ready to go home. They, or at least she, could leave soon to the Human World, but he had to get this mission underway, first. Suddenly, Matthew sat down beside Riley—quite close to him

—making Riley very uncomfortable. He forced himself not to shift in his seat.

"Sir, I ask that you do not go in to the library for the rest of the day. We are having— preparations being made for an important guest, soon, and they will be observing the library."

Ah. I guess that makes sense. Riley looked to the door, in the direction of the library. He could ask about borrowing the book he'd read last night and taking it to his room so as to not be around when the guest arrived.

"Sure! Do you mind if I get a book from there, first?"

"You may not."

The reply was so abrupt and clipped, Riley was at a loss for words.

"I say this because the guest is very interested in every book within the library. Therefore, we do not wish to displease him by taking a book out, yes?"

". . . Uh, okay. Who's the guest?"

Matthew's eyes turned steely. "Someone I doubt you know. Now, will you please stay out of the library for the sake of propriety?"

Riley blinked, searching for a good response. The best he could come up with was, "Yeah. I can. I will."

The steward, satisfied, dipped his head then went on back to his business. How strange! Why couldn't he, at least, have given Riley the name of the guest, and why did he act so defensive when Riley asked about going inside the library? No harm in asking, right? Matthew, like Lunaira, was a mystery. They both seemed to trust Caroline, but when it came to Riley? Not so much.

Oh boy. Riley headed outside to clear his brain and forget about Matthew's cryptic behavior. He spotted Edilie near the castle, in conversation with the other guards. Not wanting to attract the resentful guard's attention, Riley tiptoed into the village and hid behind a hovel. Villagers were careful to step aside as he walked past. Why were these people afraid of him? Hopefully Edilie wouldn't notice and come for him. Keeping an eye on the guard, Riley took a step forward.

"Oof!"

A scaly wall blocked his way. No, not a wall. An oversized lizard, which glared down at him with its black eyes. "Wot was dat for, ya klutz?" the creature snarled, baring its pointy little teeth at him.

"I–I—" Riley stepped back. "I'm sorry. I didn't mean to bump into you."

"Hey, Vraven," someone shouted from a stall. "Forget the kid! I still need your help over here!"

Vraven sneered at Riley and hissed, "I'd watch myself if ah were ya, keed."

Riley straightened his shoulders. He'd had enough with bullies lately. "I accidentally bumped into you. I'm sorry, okay?"

Vraven stared at him, taken aback. Growling a choice word or two under his breath, he stalked off.

Whispers circulated amongst the bystanders.

"Who is this boy?"

"Is that a star?"

"But he's a Human Worlder! How is that even possible? None of the People of the Symbol were from the Human World."

Uncomfortable with all of this attention, Riley kept his head down.

"Well now. What's this?" Edilie's derisive words reached Riley ears.

Are you serious?

"What are you doing outside the castle? Decided to cause some trouble?"

Footsteps closed in on Riley as he attempted to ignore the owner of the voice and head for the forest where he'd, hopefully, have some privacy.

"Hey, come back here, you!"

Riley started to speed up, until the clanking of armor drew closer and then a tall figure cast a shadow on the ground before him. No use trying to run. He'd probably already made the villagers even more suspicious as it was.

"Who told you that you could leave the castle, eh?"

The rest of the guards following Edilie surrounded Riley now. He was reminded of Bryan and his gang. Lifting his head, Riley gave Edilie the flattest expression he could.

"I . . . I need to go see someone."

Edilie got within inches of Riley's face and smirked. "I said, *who* told you that you could leave the castle? And who are you seeing?"

Suddenly feeling bold, Riley allowed a hint of a smirk to show on his own face. "The princess. She said I can explore. I . . . I'm going to go see Dorobonn."

Edilie's grin melted into a frown. "If you'd left the castle without permission, I would have had my men beat you senseless, and then I'd have whatever's left."

That was a revolting threat if Riley ever heard one. Not bothering to hide his disgust, Riley crossed his arms, hoping he didn't look as nervous as he felt. "I don't guess the princess would appreciate that, do you? Attacking her guests."

Edilie nodded to his men, who moved back a step or two. He snatched Riley by the shirtfront, pulling him in. "Watch your mouth, boy. Having a smart mouth will only serve to decrease your lifespan. You symbol-bearers were, and are, a bane to this world. If I could get rid of you here and now, I would." He released Riley. "See how long the princess allows you to stay at the castle. As soon as she kicks you out . . ." Edilie slid his sword in a horizontal motion across his neck.

Riley refused to comment. The reaction was satisfying, though, as Edilie walked off—brushing past him—with an icy scowl. Now he could be alone! Riley went into the forest until he could barely hear the sounds of the village and then sat down with his back to a tree. *How are my parents? Are they worried about me?* He checked his phone. No messages. *Maybe I can't get any here?*

The calm, warm atmosphere offered a sense of reprieve. Trees swayed in the breeze, which cooled him off. A dark cloud in the distance peeked over the mountains. *A storm cloud?* Riley narrowed his eyes. It didn't look like any storm cloud he'd ever seen. It had an unusual form to it, sort of serpentine-like.

Intrigued as to what might be behind the castle, Riley made his way around the outskirts of the forest surrounding the castle wall. A glance out towards the distance revealed more beautiful trees. Further on, he could just make out the green, snow-capped mountains. Forests below stretched for miles. A river flowed towards those mountains with no end in sight. A barely-discernable white area (presumably snow) shown in the south-east. To the north, the tiny outlines of another kingdom lay at the foot of a mountain. This world was similar to the paintings he'd seen in books. Beautiful and somewhat surreal.

A fog rolled in, interrupting Riley's reverie and blocking the castle from sight. The atmosphere turned eerie and . . . there was something else which made the hair on Riley's neck stand on end.

"What's going on?"

A cold rush of air stung his eyes.

I feel a menacing presence.

The disagreeable twist in his gut warned him that he was, in fact, being watched. Riley pushed to his feet. *I think I'll go.*

Even the village would probably be safer than being out here alone.

The fog thickened, as if hearing his thoughts. Where was the village?

Riley listened for the sound of people talking. Surely, the fog couldn't be so thick that it blocked noise. His blood turned to ice at a piercing screech behind him. Looking up over his shoulder, Riley spotted a bat hanging from a tree branch. A large bat. In a swirl of black mist, the bat transformed into a dark-haired man with glacial blue eyes and a fang jutting out from the top left side of his mouth—the same man Riley had seen at his house.

Oh, no! The bloodpire!

The bloodpire grinned at Riley. His eyes glittered with venomous delight.

"Well, well, well. If it isn't the boy I met just yesterday," he purred.

Riley poised himself for a fight.

"What are you doing out here, little one? Surely you realize how dangerous this world is for someone like you?"

"Someone like *me*? What do you mean by that? Who are you anyway?"

"I am Glazhier. I lived with the Bloodpire Clan for years until I was banished. Banished for . . . unlawful behavior." Glazhier pointed at Riley's star. "You have a symbol. Do you not know how risky it is for you to be out here? And with a star, no less? People will wish to imprison you, or perhaps even . . . destroy you."

"You mean people like *you*?" Riley's hands buzzed. Tiny currents of red electricity traveled up and down his palms.

The bloodpire merely grunted. "Quite right. You may as well go ahead and consider your life forfeit."

Riley lifted his hands, prepared to shoot lightning if

Glazhier suddenly charged. "I remember you telling me to stay out of your business. What did you mean by that?"

Glazhier's eyes flashed. So malicious was his gaze, it made Riley shudder. "There is someone I'm after. My quarry. If you dare help him, I will make your death slow and painful."

Why? Who's this "quarry"? He didn't have a chance to ask, for Glazhier shouted, "Mídian!" and a streak of dark indigo lightning sped at Riley.

He dropped to the ground with an "oof!" as the lightning passed over his head.

The bloodpire snarled. He sent another bolt for Riley, who rolled out of the way. Jumping up, Riley dashed into the fog. Behind him, Glazhier screeched with such blood-curdling intensity, Riley refused to slow down, not caring what direction he ran, as long as it was away from Glazhier. He wouldn't stop, couldn't stop—

He nearly crashed into another boy.

A couple of inches shorter than Riley, the boy had blonde hair, blue eyes that practically glowed, and . . . a fang on the right side of his mouth.

He seemed to be about fifteen and wore a gray shirt, brown pants, and leather shoes. A set of velvety-textured, dark gray wings protruded from the boy's back. Unfurled, they went past his shoulders by a good three feet.

Another bloodpire?

Chapter Nine

Riley stumbled back. "A-are you a bloodpire, too?"

"What?" The boy cocked a brow. "No. I'm a vampire. My name's Joseph." He frowned. "What do you mean 'too'?"

Riley didn't know if that was any better than a bloodpire, but he didn't know who else to turn to for help. "I need to get outta here. There's a bloodpire chasing me!"

"A bloodpire? Who?" As soon as he said that, Joseph looked past Riley and gasped.

Riley spun around, and saw Glazhier staring them down with a cruel smile.

"Him!" Riley exclaimed, noting how Joseph paled at the sight of the bloodpire. Wait, could this guy be the one Glazhier was after?

It seemed so, for Glazhier's expression changed into that of a hunter who'd cornered his prey and wanted to play with it before striking. He pointed at Joseph and said, "I have been searching for *you*!" His skeletal finger glowed red. "Now I can have fun eradicating *two* victims!"

"C'mon!" Joseph grabbed Riley's wrist and pulled him along. A blast of fire enveloped the area where they'd stood only seconds ago. "We'll head for the village! Glazhier despises it!"

Riley gave no answer, but allowed Joseph to lead the way. He stole a glimpse behind him, but did not see Glazhier. Upon making it into the village, they hid behind a hovel where Joseph told Riley to stay while he looked around the corner and scanned the village.

"I didn't see him. Maybe he left?" Riley said quietly.

"Possibly. Glazhier's known for his stealth, however." Eventually, Joseph plopped down next to Riley and sighed. "That was close. Glazhier's relentless."

Riley started to ask why Glazhier was after Joseph, when a portly man with unkempt hair and an apron showed up to grab a barrel from a stack beside them. He nearly dropped it the minute he saw the two boys. "Wha' in the world a' you kids doin' here? This is no place for loitering. Go on!"

Joseph held up his hands in defense. "We're sorry, sir. We were . . . playing a game and thought we could hide here."

The man opened his mouth to shout, but then squinted his eyes at Joseph, and drew closer. The little vampire stepped back, wary. The man's eyes popped open. He unexpectedly poked a chubby finger into Joseph's chest, saying, "'Ey, now. *you're* that blithering young fellow who caused that bloodpire to ruin my stall, aren't you?" Recognition swept across Joseph's face, which was then replaced by guilt. When he didn't respond, the man jabbed his finger into Joseph's chest, pushing the little guy into a pole holding up the awning connected to the house. "Aren't you? Speak up, boy!" Seeing Joseph pinned between this man's finger and the pole, Riley's temper flared. Joseph didn't need this guy coming at him, after what happened with Glazhier.

"Hey, leave him alone!"

The man directed his anger—now in full swing—at Riley and jabbed his finger into Riley's chest. "Ah! *You're* the boy with the star. A danger to society. Our village has gone through enough without *your* kind here." He lowered his hand, glaring at the both of them. "You kids don't belong here. So, I suggest you get out before I have you arrested."

Joseph bowed his head. "Yes, sir. I'm sorry." Apparently satisfied with Joseph's reply, the man hobbled off, having forgotten about the barrel. Riley scowled at his back. What had the People of the Symbol done to infuriate these villagers? Needless to say, what did he mean about Joseph causing Glazhier to ruin his stall? Something tugged at his shirtsleeve.

"Hurry. Let's go." Joseph gestured to the forest.

"Where are we going?" Riley asked warily. "Where are you taking me?"

"My friend and I can help you! He's a mizzer. His name's Kelvin," Joseph explained, letting go of Riley's shirt.

"What's a mizzer? How can he help me?"

"I'll explain later!" Joseph whispered.

They crept through the forest before Joseph halted behind an abandoned cabin on the west side of the village. A young man, who looked to be about seventeen years of age, sat on a stone outcrop not far from the cabin. He wore a red vest and white shirt with the sleeves rolled up, along with brown breeches and black leather shoes. His skin had a deep tan, as if he spent most of his time in the sun. He appeared more similar to a Human Worlder than some of the creatures from this world. A hat sat on the stone beside him, and his short, dark hair stuck out in every direction.

"Hey!" the young man greeted them.

"Kelvin!" Joseph shouted and then pointed at Riley. "He needs our help!"

Kelvin grabbed his hat, clambered down the stones like a cat, and then jumped, landing flat on his feet without so much as a grunt. When he straightened, he stood just a little taller than Riley. His brown eyes revealed a playful disposition, and his smile, easy-going.

"So, what's up?" Kelvin mussed Joseph's hair like an older brother might.

"Glazhier is chasing him." The little vampire peered over his shoulder, cautious. "We need to go. Glazhier might be on to us."

Kelvin's eyes widened. "Got it!"

"So, mate," Kelvin said, elbowing Riley companionably (if a bit hard) in the side, "what're you doing here? I've never seen you before."

"I'm here to stop the Dark Magic," Riley explained. Admittedly, a bit of an odd way to begin a conversation, but it was the best he could do, what with the current circumstances. "Glazhier said that my star puts my life in danger and that . . ." He glanced at Joseph, not wanting the younger boy to hear his next comment. However, Kelvin seemed to not need an explanation. He noticed where Riley's gaze landed and jerked a stiff nod. More than likely, he knew about Joseph and Glazhier's conflict.

"We'll head for our hiding place near the Endless Field. Glazhier's never found it," Joseph said.

"Near the what?" Riley's mind spun with all these names.

Kelvin and Joseph looked at him curiously. "The Endless Field," the mizzer said. "Didntcha know?"

"Er . . ." Riley cleared his throat and then scuffed the ground with his foot. "I'm not actually from here. I'm from the Human World." All went silent. Kelvin and Joseph's stares of disbelief were enough to make Riley want to sink into the ground. His ears rang, drowning out the sounds of the forest.

"You're from the Human World?" Joseph squeaked. "But . . . how did you get here?"

"Through a door in the forest," Riley explained, growing tired of having to tell everyone he encountered his situation. It made him feel like an intruder.

Kelvin narrowed his eyes. "Then . . . how come you have a star? Only the People of the Symbol had symbols, and they were from this world."

Riley shrugged. "It just appeared. I can't really tell you how."

Kelvin and Joseph glanced at each other, amazed. "Wow, mate!" Kelvin exclaimed. "You can tell us more when we get to the hiding place."

"So, how . . . how far is this hiding place?" Riley asked, hoping these guys were trustworthy. *I guess they would've already beaten me up if they weren't.*

"We're almost there," Kelvin replied. "Is everything alright?"

Riley managed to hold back a flinch. Was his discomfort that obvious? "Err, yeah. I'm fine. I was just curious. Princess Lunaira is letting my friend and me stay at the castle." He could've kicked himself. Why did he tell these guys where he was staying?

"Really? Well, isn't that great?" Kelvin said, thumping Riley on the back, almost knocking the breath out of him.

Riley coughed, disguising it as a laugh. "Yep. Sure is." Although the question of whether or not these guys were trustworthy, continued nagging at him.

"So, Kelvin, what's a mizzer?"

"They're . . . how do I put this? They're all a part of their own groups. The one I used to be a part of isn't the only one out there. If there's one thing they like—it's causing pain. I left because I couldn't stand what they were doing. I've seen them beat some fella up because he wouldn't join our gang. Heck, I sure couldn't blame him."

"Wow," Riley whistled, hoping he never encountered one. Well, with Kelvin being the exception.

"What did the guy do? The one they roughed up?"

"He had guts, I'll give him that. He refused to join and, eventually, Marcus—he's the leader—relented and left him for dead. I took the fella to a nearby village where they could help him. They had a healer of sorts there."

Riley had to admit it. Kelvin also had guts. To possibly risk his life and save a stranger from a gang was more than he could imagine doing. He'd helped Max, but not at the expense of his life, although it'd felt like it at the time.

"Dude, you're bold."

A funny look from Kelvin told him the mizzer had no earthly idea what he just said.

"'Dude'?"

"It's . . . aaahh. It's a word we say in the Human World."

"What does it mean?"

"It's like calling someone . . . like calling someone 'mate'."

Kelvin narrowed his eyes, making Riley think that he'd said something wrong. "Interesting. What other words are there?"

"Um. Let's see. There are lots more."

"Shhh!" Riley and Kelvin both started at Joseph's hiss for them to be quiet. He crouched behind a small boulder, about ten feet ahead, and motioned for them to lay low. Riley and Kelvin glanced at each other before doing as Joseph instructed. They caught up to Joseph, who pointed over the boulder. Riley peered around the corner and noticed the bloodpire, Glazhier. He wasn't doing anything. Thankfully, his back was to them. Wait. A little blue wisp of smoke circled his body and then landed in his gaunt hand.

"Revenge will be sweet when I get my hands on that puny vampire."

Riley nearly gasped. What was Glazhier's deal with Joseph? Why did he despise the little guy so much?

"I'll make sure to give him a nice and slow death. Agonizingly slow. Those fools in the Bloodpire Clan Council believed his words that I murdered another bloodpire. My lie couldn't convince them otherwise." He let out an animal-like snarl that made Riley cringe. "I'll make him pay. He'll be sorry. Oh, so sorry!" The bloodpire transformed into a bat and flew off, screeching for all the world to hear.

Riley and Kelvin turned to Joseph, who thumped his forehead to the boulder.

"Boy. Was it ever a mistake to do that," he muttered, evidently not expecting a response.

"Do what?" Riley inquired, sitting beside Joseph. "What's Glazhier's problem?"

Joseph situated himself with his back to the boulder and leaned his head against it. Staring at the sky, he gulped. "He . . . I . . ." Joseph groaned and rubbed his face with his palms. "I witnessed him murdering a bloodpire that he'd been arguing with. The poor fellow didn't stand a chance. It was a stupid argument that Glazhier initiated. I'd . . . rather not say what he did." Joseph tugged at his collar, clearly disturbed. "I . . . I asked for permission to talk to the leader of the bloodpires. My clan doesn't even know. Our clans don't get along, and so I knew what they'd say. Therefore, I went alone. Surprisingly, they were open to listening to a vampire. Not only that, but a vampire *kid*. At least, that's how Glazhier put it. He was furious. He kept saying the bloodpires were fool enough to listen to a little snitch of a vampire who was nothing but a pain.

'You'd rather listen to this *boy* This *kid*?!' he roared. I remember." Joseph chuckled humorlessly. "Soon after they banished him, Glazhier looked at me which such—such a terrifying stare. I've never so scared in my life! He said to me, 'when I get my hands on you, you'll wish you were dead instead of having to face me.'"

Riley listened quietly. Poor Joseph, he was only trying to do the right thing. He could certainly empathize with him. Kelvin put a hand on Joseph's shoulder.

"C'mon, mate. Let's go to the village. That'll be the safest place for now."

Joseph smiled weakly. "Good idea." He turned to Riley. "You can come with us. That way you'll make it to the castle before dark. None of us are safe from Glazhier here."

Riley agreed. He needed to talk to Caroline as well. Joseph was already ahead of them when Kelvin blocked Riley's path.

"Can I ask you something?"

For a split second, Riley was suspicious of what Kelvin might say. Or do, for that matter, but he didn't want to jump to conclusions. "Sure. What's up?"

What he didn't expect was for Kelvin's eyes to dim and his tone to get lower. "Joseph is like a little brother to me. I don't want him hurt. If you're going to hang out with us, you need to promise to help me protect him." He poked his finger into Riley's chest. "I think you could be a good friend, but you need to earn that trust, mate."

Earn that trust. Riley could do that, no problem. And in the meantime, whatever magic he learned to help defend himself from Iradocc would be beneficial in helping to keep Joseph safe from Glazhier. He held out his hand, saying, "You've got my word. Mate." To his pleasant surprise, Kelvin understood the gesture. He took Riley's hand in his and gave it a firm shake. Riley forced back a wince. This guy had quite the grip.

Chapter Ten

Once they arrived at the village, Riley, Kelvin, and Joseph went their separate ways, promising to meet up later. Shouts from deeper within the village piqued Riley's curiosity. The commotion had attracted a fair-sized crowd and some people from the crowd were laughing. Unfortunately, the laughter didn't have a very friendly ring to it. Riley stood on his tiptoes to see what was going on.

"If you can't pay the money, urchin, then ya gotta leave!" the stall-keeper—who was the one shouting—said, jabbing a long finger at a young red-headed boy of about twelve years old.

Not everyone laughed, but no one defended the kid or did anything to help him.

"But sir, I can go get the money from my mother. It's my little brother's birthday and I don't have anything for him," the boy said, "and I was hoping to get him a slingshot." He slid the two coins on the counter to the owner and pointed at a row of wooden slingshots hanging from a wall in the back. "I can't afford anything else. I'll ask my mother for some money and then will return. How is that too much trouble?"

Picking up the coins, the stall-keeper inspected them. "Listen, boy, you're just holding up my business. It'll take too long for you to go to your mother and ask for the money. I don't have time to wait."

"You don't have to!" the kid exclaimed. "I can just wait my turn. That's fine."

The stall-keeper sneered. "I'm already tired of even seeing you around here. You're not worth anyone's time. You're nothing but a pesky nobody." With that, he stretched out his arm and shoved the boy back, hard.

The kid landed with a thud, much to the amusement of several in the crowd—the wind knocked out of him. No one lent a hand to help him up. They even moved out of the way, as if he had some sort of disease. Riley's face grew hot. He'd already promised himself that he wouldn't stand by and just watch someone get picked on. He squeezed his way through. It wasn't terribly difficult, since anyone who took a good look at him as they turned to glare, moved out of the way, instantly. The kid got up and said, "Sir, please!"

Riley stood beside the boy and put a hand on his shoulder. He then looked at the stall-keeper. "Hey. You know, you should either give him back his coins if you don't want him buying from you, or let him go and get whatever he needs in order to buy something."

The stall-keeper ignored Riley's presence for a little while and then lazily faced him. "Is that so?" The stall-keeper tucked the coins into his pocket. "And what makes *you* the boss, eh?"

"What you're doing is wrong, and you know it. Give him back his coins or let him buy one of those slingshots." Riley maintained eye contact with the stall-keeper who actually seemed astonished at his insistence. It quickly changed into fury as he pointed a finger at Riley. "Who do you think you are, boy? You're doing something mighty risky by ordering me to give those coins back."

Behind Riley, the villagers murmured. Was it Riley's imagination, or did more people join in on the spectacle? The suspicion from earlier grew into frustration. He could see it in their eyes. He could hear the whispers. Who was this boy to disrupt their way of life? So what if the stall-keeper didn't give the little scamp a slingshot? It was survival among the fittest here. If you couldn't afford something, you were out—no excuses.

"As I said, you can't just take his money from him! If he can't pay for the slingshot, you give the coins back," Riley protested, keeping an eye on the crowd.

"I can do whatever pleases me. Hold up." The stall-keeper's eyes flashed. "You have a star!"

A flush crept up Riley's collar. Prickles ran down his neck at the sensation of being watched. Not by the crowd, but by an unwanted presence.

"How is this possible that you have a star?" the stall-keeper said in a not-so-quiet tone. "All of the People of the Symbol were eradicated years ago. I hear you're from the Human World. Is that true?"

If he only needed to stand up to this man, Riley would have no problem. Being encircled by a skittish crowd, on the other hand . . .

Who knew what they'd do if they decided to attack?

The man leaned towards Riley, growling, "Answer me, boy. Are you from the Human World?"

The people murmured to each other, all in agreement. The kid got closer to Riley, just in case.

"He is from de Human World! I overheard de guards talking about him," a nasally voice interrupted. It was the oversized reptile from earlier. He pushed through to the inner edges of the crowd. What was his name again? Gavin? He pointed a finger at Riley.

"He's a troublemaker, dat one!"

Thunder rumbled in the far distance to the south. The stall-keeper exclaimed, "Hear that? He must be doing this!" The warmth in the air dissipated, replaced by a coolness one would experience during a winter storm.

"What're you talking about? It's a storm. They happen. I'm not causing it!" Riley searched frantically for a way out. The crowd seemed to thicken as they closed in on him. He needed to get the red-headed kid to safety, but how?

"The star is dangerous! People with symbols always bring bad luck! On top of that, Human Worlders have only brought destruction to our world!" someone shouted.

"Dey're right!" the reptile said. "We all know what a bane people with symbols are, and we can't risk having more Human Worlders walking among us."

Riley clenched his fists. All this talk about how people with symbols were dangerous, and yet he was given no explanation whatsoever. Not to mention, Human Worlders were also looked down upon. "Look! Err, Gavin—"

"De name's *Vraven*!"

"Sorry. V-Vraven. What do you mean by saying that people with symbols are dangerous? And what have Human Worlders done to you?"

Vraven bared his teeth. "Because of you, strange things are happening. That cloud—" he pointed at the sky—"for one. It appeared not long before you came. That means it must've been an omen. Any time a person with a symbol came into the kingdom, disasters happened. As for Human Worlders, they came and tried to steal our livelihoods from us."

Riley considered this. "How many Human Worlders have you had?"

"More than we want," the stall-keeper growled.

That doesn't necessarily answer my question. That could mean one or one hundred Human Worlders.

". . . How do you know the disasters happened because of the People of the Symbol? Iradocc—who later destroyed them—could've made it so that whenever one of them traveled anywhere, a catastrophe happened. Therefore, everyone thought the person with the symbol was causing it, but that person was truly innocent." Could that be why these people were more or less known to history? They hid themselves away because everyone shunned them, thinking they brought bad luck?

This idea made the crowd stir. Most knew that Iradocc could not be trusted and it was said that Dark Magic could be used to control others. What if the boy was right?

"And yet, you're a Human Worlder," a man on Riley's left said. "You may have a symbol, but how do we know *you* wouldn't cause the same trouble as the other Human Worlders?"

Riley scanned the crowd, praying for the right words to speak. "I . . . I'm not a mischief maker. The only way I can prove this to you is by helping you. I am here to save Zefa from Iradocc."

The confused reactions unsettled him. Iradocc was coming to Zefa? Why? Could it be that this boy was the reason for Iradocc's arrival? This revelation sent animosity coursing through their veins. They didn't bother thinking about Riley's promise to rescue them, however.

"Imprison the boy!" a villager shouted. "He's why Iradocc will invade the kingdom! Lock him in the cells!"

What Riley intended for bringing the villagers hope, merely served to anger them. The crowd didn't argue with the suggestion to lock him up. In fact, they agreed! Riley wracked his brain for a solution. Could he and the kid outrun the mob? Not with so many surrounding them and the stall behind them.

"Enough!"

The people stopped in their tracks, baffled, except for the little boy, who appeared to recognize the voice, for he brightened the moment he heard it. The crowd broke, allowing a man with emerald-green eyes into the circle.

Dorobonn!

Both the stall-keeper and Vraven were none too happy to see the older magician. The stall-keeper bristled. "What're you doing here, sorcerer? Are you here to defend this miscreant whose very presence portends disaster?"

Dorobonn got behind Riley and the little boy with a hand on each's shoulder. "This young man and this child are none of your concern. You will leave them alone."

Vraven hissed, turning malicious eyes on Riley. "That boy should be in da cells for even being here." The stall-keeper stepped up as well and looked at the little red-head before sneering at Dorobonn.

"You care for those who don't matter to any of us. Why should he matter to you?"

Dorobonn's eyes glinted. If Riley didn't know any better, he'd say the stall-keeper and Vraven actually seemed a bit scared of Dorobonn. If for a moment. "I care for those who cannot defend themselves. This boy—" he patted Riley's shoulder, "is no menace to the village. Dark Magic is the true menace. This lad will be the one to save you all, just as he said. In the meantime, do not bother either of them."

The people watched in disapproval, and someone muttered, "That magician is taking the boy under his wing. Have you ever seen anything so irresponsible?"

Neither Vraven nor the stall-keeper said anything more. Dorobonn handed the stall-keeper a few coins and asked for a slingshot, somehow knowing the little red-head wanted one. The stall-keeper reluctantly acquiesced. Vraven grumbled something under his breath and then walked away. At last, the crowd dispersed.

"Come, Riley," Dorobonn said. "I need to speak with you. Away from here."

Gladly! As Riley followed Dorobonn, he had that uncomfortable feeling again that he was being watched. He looked over his shoulder, but saw no one. He'd felt an unnatural presence earlier, but couldn't pinpoint who or where it came from. While trying to figure that out, Riley caught sight of the stall-keeper talking to Edilie. The stall-keeper pointed at Riley, and when the guard made eye contact with him, he frowned. Jerking a nod at his men, they marched towards Riley.

Oh no. After his earlier confrontation with Edilie, Riley had no desire to go through that again.

Wait. Where's Dorobonn? The magician had disappeared in to the horde of villagers.

Riley would need to lose himself in the crowd to avoid Edilie. That wasn't easy, as people threw him disgusted looks and kept their distance. This, without a doubt, made matters worse. He hid behind a hovel with his back to a barrel, hoping Edilie would pass by without searching too carefully. He heard footsteps, and then they stopped. Eventually, the guard grumbled and he and his men headed in the opposite direction. Sighing in relief, Riley peeked around the corner of the small home.

Where could Dorobonn be?

Chapter Eleven

Riley made it to the edge of the village, hoping he'd be able to spot Dorobonn or the red-head. No luck. How could Dorobonn have gotten so far in such a short amount of time? Careful to avoid the stall-keeper and Vraven, Riley crept out from behind the hovel and snuck into the forest, which was close by, as quietly as possible. Going deeper, Riley examined the area, turning his head this way and that, hoping he wouldn't encounter Glazhier. Not only that, but where did Dorobonn live? Sitting on a stump, Riley exhaled a long breath. He had no idea what he was supposed to do right now. Obviously, going to Dorobonn's home was out of the question. He feared asking anyone if they knew where Dorobonn lived. They might report him to Edilie.

A hand touched his shoulder.

"Oh my—!" He whipped around, thinking Edilie had tracked him down.

Joseph backed off a few steps, holding up his hands in a peace gesture.

"Sorry to scare you. I didn't know if something was wrong."

"No. No, you're fine. I thought . . . I thought you were the guard, Edilie."

The vampire glanced over his shoulder and then back at Riley. "I'm constantly on the lookout for Glazhier, so I understand. Hey, so, Kelvin and I wanted to show you our hideout. Unless, of course, you're busy. I remember you saying you had some business to attend to at the castle."

Riley snorted. Yeah, he was busy. Busy staying away from everyone who wanted to imprison him! Gathering his composure, Riley stood up and cuffed Joseph on the arm.

"Sure thing! I'll . . . I'll go to the castle later."

Joseph cocked a brow. "You're certain?"

"Totally. Let's go!" The word "totally" seemed lost on Joseph, for the blank expression on his face spoke volumes. Either that, or Riley's sudden enthusiasm. Or both.

"Allllright, then. Come with me," Joseph said. "Kelvin is already there. It's is in the forest—this way, next to a riverbed." They made their way through the forest and over an outcrop of boulders. Climbing gingerly, Riley took a bit longer, as there weren't many places for him to get a good grip. Finally, they made it to a beautiful area in the midst of the trees. The air smelled damp, but there wasn't a cloud in the sky—save the storm cloud further off. Riley heard the sound of rushing water. The foliage grew lush and deep green. Moss blanketed the lower part of the trees, and tiny little mushrooms dotted the trunks. A miniscule flicker zoomed by in Riley's periphery, and he wondered if any fairies lived in these forests. After reading about them in a few of the books he owned, the idea made him curious.

At last, they reached the river. There, Kelvin sat on a log bridge with his legs dangling over the water. He held a piece of wood in one hand and a knife in the other, which he used to strip away the bark.

"Kelvin! Look who came along."

The mizzer looked up from his work, and his eyes lit up when he saw Riley.

"Hey, hey, if it isn't the fella with the star." Kelvin tossed the piece of wood and knife towards the bank and stood up. He made his way across the log, to where Riley and Joseph stood. "So, what brings you here?"

"Joseph invited me to see your hideout." Riley stared at the river. "This is super neat!"

Kelvin smiled. "Thanks. There's also a canopy further on. We could show it to you right now if you'd like?"

Riley nodded.

The trees grew taller as they walked, and the foliage, lighter green. Sunlight poured through the leaves, creating a greenish tint. They came upon a shelter of small trees, which were barely taller than Riley's head, clustered together. However, the roots were all so tangled up, they formed thick "seats," allowing one to sit on them.

Joseph sat on a single large root. The moss atop the roots actually made them rather comfortable.

Kelvin handed the wood he'd been whittling to Riley. "Ever done this before, mate?"

Riley shrugged. "Umm, a few times."

"Here." Kelvin handed him the knife. "Try it. I've been workin' on making a spear."

Riley slowly slid the knife across the rough surface.

"Do you, perchance, know what happened in the village earlier? Joe, here, says that a lot of people were shouting and acting up. He also saw—whom he thought to be you—protecting a little kid from a stall-keeper and that pain in the neck, Vraven. He also said he heard them accusing you of trying to destroy us?" Kelvin said.

Riley hoped his new friends didn't believe the accusations

the villagers kept throwing at him. "Err, yeah. They said that people with symbols are bad luck and that the cloud heading this way is because of me. It's not! I can tell you that for a fact. Also, they said that other Human Worlders have come and wreaked havoc on their township."

Kelvin tapped a finger to his chin, contemplating these claims. "Hm. I don't recall any Human Worlders having done anything bad. That doesn't mean something bad hasn't happened."

"They're blaming you for the alleged actions of those who came before you," Joseph stated. "They're also saying that since one or more Human Worlders did wicked things, means that all of them are the same—which is nonsense. There are plenty of Zefans who are questionable as well."

I doubt that crosses their minds. Riley rubbed his face with his hand. How could he convince these people that he was on their side?

"By the way. Do you guys know of a man named Dorobonn?"

Kelvin and Joseph exchanged glances. Neither had any clue who Riley was talking about.

"What does he look like?" Joseph inquired.

"He's . . . well . . . he's pretty tall. Older. He has green eyes, and wears a cape."

Kelvin shook his head. "Sorry, mate. I don't recall anyone like that."

"Nor I," Joseph said. How could that be? Even Lunaira wasn't able to give him a solid answer when he'd asked her about Dorobonn. Was the guy really that elusive?

"Why? Are you searching for him?" Kelvin asked.

"Um. Yeah. He said he wanted to talk to me . . . but I don't know where he lives."

"Have you met this fella before?"

"Yeah. In the Human World."

"But he didn't tell you where he lived?"

Riley shrugged. "No. I was supposed to follow him after that whole commotion in the village, but then got separated."

"Tough luck, mate. But we'll help you look for him."

Riley chuckled. Kelvin sure had a way of speaking bluntly. "Thanks, guys."

"By the way, what's this 'guys' word you use?" Joseph replied.

"It's like saying 'fellas.' It's a word we use in the Human World."

"What strange words you Human Worlders have. Hehe, you gonna continue working on that spear, or what?" Kelvin joked, pointing at the blunt piece of wood in Riley's hand.

"Ah, right." Riley shaved off some more bark, remembering how he and his brothers used to do this. Terry was always better at it. Riley's usually ended up rough and not as sharp, or too narrow since he'd shave too much off.

"Had my ears deceived me, or did you say you're here in Leíso to stop Dark Magic?" Kelvin said.

"Yep. That I am." The more Riley thought about it, the more nervous he became.

"Do you know magic?"

"I overheard someone say you do," Joseph explained.

"Errr, well . . ." The red spark that had appeared in his hand after reading that book in the castle's library came to mind. "I . . . I've never actually used it before. I've read words that—for lack of a better way of saying it—cause magic."

"I suppose it would make sense to know magic in order to battle magic," Kelvin observed.

If that's true, help me, Elomé. Dorobonn knew magic. Maybe that's why he'd told Riley to come with him! To teach

Riley magic and help him understand how to use that knowledge.

"I also know magic," Joseph said.

"You do?" Riley exclaimed.

"Yeah. Well . . . sort of. I have the ability to stop things and people in whatever they're doing. The thing is, I can only use my ability for so long and so often. The more I use it, the more it hurts me. I grow tired if I do it for too long." Even talking about his ability appeared to make Joseph uncomfortable.

"That's cool!" Feeling awkward at the abrupt end of the conversation, Riley lifted the stick he'd been whittling. "What do you guys think?" He handed it to Kelvin, watching as his friend analyzed it; inspecting its sharpness by tapping the tip. Riley placed his elbows on his knees, noting Kelvin's thoughtful expression.

"I gotta say, mate, I'm impressed. You did well. If you'd like, you can take it with you. You probably wouldn't be able to use it in a fight, but at least it looks . . . neat? That's one of the Human World words you used, right?"

Riley laughed. "Yeah. And that's fine. It can just stay here. It can be a fun decoration."

He heard a rustling sound and turned his head. Joseph's wings were quivering. The little vampire was just as puzzled as Riley felt.

"Joe. What's goin' on with your wings?" Kelvin asked.

Joseph shook his head, his eyes going wide. "I don't know. They've never done this before. At least, not that I recall." He stood up and touched them. The surface rippled and lurched at the contact.

Soon after, the atmosphere grew eerie.

Kelvin's jaw tightened. "C'mon," he said. "Let's get out of here."

They prepared to leave, but Riley couldn't shake the

discomfort he was feeling. Something was wrong. Riley couldn't think clearly. A wisp of mist slithered along the ground and then curled around his arm. As the mist spread over his hand, his stomach dropped.

Mesmerized, Riley stared as the mist snaked through the openings of his fingers and branched out over his palm.

What's going on?! Out of nowhere, Riley felt, what seemed like a hand, jerking him back, pulling him out of his stupor. He shook his arm and the mist evaporated. No one was there, so what had woken him up? A sharp pain stung his temple. *"There is nowhere you can go that I will not be, boy."* The words pounded his skull, making it impossible to focus.

"Kelvin? Joseph?" He couldn't see them anywhere. "Where are you guys?" The forest spun, and Riley fought to keep his balance.

A hand—an actual hand caught his arm before he fell to the ground.

"Riley! Are you okay?"

Kelvin's voice. Riley sat on the ground, holding his head in his hands, attempting to stop the spinning. Kelvin and Joseph knelt in front of him, their faces full of concern.

"Where'd you—where'd you guys go?" Riley stuttered.

The two exchanged glances. "We didn't go anywhere," Joseph replied. "You were acting odd and almost passed out. We did answer you."

Riley's brain couldn't process this. Whose voice had he heard in his head? It'd been inhuman . . . frightening.

"But I couldn't see you guys." Riley's face flushed. "I think . . . I need to go back to the village."

Kelvin nodded his head, wary. "Okay. We'll come with you until we reach the castle. Don't want you fainting on the way, mate." As they walked away from the grove of trees in silence, Riley thought he heard a malevolent chuckle.

Chapter Twelve

The three friends bid each other goodbye soon after reaching the castle. Sweat dampened Riley's palms as he gazed at the village. Edilie stood guard at the castle's entrance. Having no desire to confront the guard, Riley hung back in the forest.

I've got to find Dorobonn. Late evening crept upon the kingdom. He also needed to be careful.

Holding his hand up, Riley flexed his fingers and whispered, "gaphladeen." Thin branches of red electricity spread through his skin. He could see the outlines of the static. It felt strange. Riley closed his hand, ignoring the growing intensity of the heat. His skin pulsed within his fist. His fingers stung, as if they'd fallen asleep. He opened his hand and, like looking into a kaleidoscope, the electricity flowed and ebbed, in and out.

What was one of the other words I'd read?

It started with a "p"; that much he was sure of.

"P . . . pale–no . . . pald . . . no. Pal. Pallllllstona!" His palm glowed yellow and it tickled. Riley laughed softly. A tiny sparkle floated just above the center. It grew until it was the size of a baseball. A glittering baseball. Mesmerized, Riley touched it with the tip of his finger. A shock traveled through his arm.

"Ouch!" If this magic was coming from his own body, why did it hurt him? Shouldn't he be immune to it? At least, that was his logic. He had no idea how magic worked.

How do I find out where Dorobonn lives? He can help me, no doubt.

He made to close his hand. The sparkling sphere stayed put, much to Riley's annoyance and discomfort. He snapped his wrist and the sphere flew through the air and burst when it hit a tree. A scorch mark branded the trunk. *Oops.* The forest—so silent a mere breath would disrupt the peace—tempted him to venture deeper and uncover whatever mysteries they held. Riley inhaled deeply and turned away. He could hear rumbles of thunder coming from the mountain ranges, and the atmosphere felt heavy.

"Hey, yer the one with the star, arentcha?" said a greasy voice at the edge of the village.

Riley turned. Four unusual rodent-looking creatures observed him from beneath the cover of low-hanging branches, their eyes glowing green in the shadows.

"Uhh, yeah sure," Riley said, unable to help noticing their rat-like appearances. "Who are you?"

"We're gnavrs, boy," the one who'd addressed him responded, showing his teeth. "Don't ya know it's rude to stare?"

Riley shrugged. "Err, I'm sorry." He needed to get out of here!

The gnavr sauntered up to him and blocked his path. "Everyone's heard aboutcha," the gnavr said, pointing a claw at Riley. "We saw you just now practicing magic. You'd better watch where you use that stuff." The gnavr nodded towards the village. "There's been a commotion throughout the village about you. D'ya know anything about that?" His rat-eyes gleamed ominously.

"Umm, well . . . I can imagine. Look, I need to go, okay? I have friends waiting for me." The realization that someone had been watching him, made Riley more uncomfortable than ever. As he was trying to walk away, he tripped on a tree root and before Riley could catch himself, he brushed against the gnavr.

The gnavr grabbed Riley. "What was that for, ya little delinquent?"

"Whoa! It was an accident! I'm sorry." Riley wanted to shove the creature aside, but who knew what this creature could do to him?

The gnavr's lip curled. "Ya think since ya have a star, you have a right ta push me around?"

What? "No, it . . . was an accident, I'm telling you," Riley insisted.

The gnavr's friends smirked. "Tear 'im up, Goblar!" one of them hooted. "Teach 'im a lesson!"

"Good idea." Goblar lifted his claws and hissed, "Yer kind isn't welcome here, kid. Yer star is a curse. I'll rip ya apart!"

Riley shut his eyes, but the claws never touched him. When Riley peeked, he nearly passed out with relief. Dorobonn stood there with a tight clasp on the creature's wrist.

"I was wondering where you were," the magician said with a kind smile. It disappeared the second he looked at the creature.

"You will not harm the boy. If you do, I shall have no choice but to keep you as far from him as necessary. And it will not be pleasant."

The gnavr let go of Riley, turning his disdain on Dorobonn. "Oh, really? And what're ya gonna do, huh? Yer just an old magician. You can't scare me!" Goblar pointed a claw at Dorobonn's chest.

The magician, on the other hand, looked more unimpressed with the insult than angry.

"I suggest you do not try anything foolish then, gnavr. Make your choices wisely," Dorobonn advised and glanced at the creature's companions.

Goblar seethed and flexed his claws. Dorobonn stared him in the eye.

Reluctantly, Goblar cowed away and gestured for his friends.

"You can't protect that boy." He stabbed a claw at Riley. "We will all die because of him!"

"What're you talking about?" Riley's brain spun with all the accusations these Zefans had been giving him as of late.

Goblar sneered. "You will destroy us with your magic. You symbol is a danger to us all." His tone darkened. "You cannot be allowed to live."

"Ióna!" Dorobonn made a circular motion with his fingers, effectively sealing the creature's mouth shut. Goblar clawed at his mouth, alarmed. His friends squawked in terror and ran. He shrank back as Dorobonn marched up to him.

"Your claims against the boy are not true," Dorobonn said "—and you can tell your companions that they can keep their superstitions to themselves, or I will stretch all of your tails and tie them over your mouths."

Goblar nodded vigorously then staggered after the others. The moment they were gone, Riley smiled in gratitude at Dorobonn, who guided him onward with a hand on his back. "Thanks for that, Dorobonn. I don't know what I would've done."

Dorobonn chuckled. "It seems you have a habit of getting

yourself into trouble, young one. I am impressed, however, with the way you handled the situation."

Riley didn't think so. There were several ways he could've handled it better, he was sure. All the same, he accepted Dorobonn's compliment.

"What is the matter, Riley? You look uncertain."

One thing could be said for Dorobonn—this guy undoubtedly had a keen eye.

"I . . . I just think I could've done something different. I freaked out and didn't even think to use my magic."

"If you had used your magic, then it would have attracted unwanted attention, more than likely. The Dark Magic is slowly making its way into other's hearts within this kingdom. Althia is not a large kingdom. You must be more careful around here. Zefa was once a peaceful village, but people became more and more fearful and suspicious once the Dark Magic invaded. The prophecy of a third star-bearer defeating Iradocc has them frightened and uncertain. He has placed a superstition in the hearts of the weak that the one with the symbol will be their demise," Dorobonn said. "The entire kingdom is now under quiet chaos as the Dark Magic seeps in." His voice turned solemn. "Goblar believes that your star is a danger to him, and others in Zefa. Your mission is, not only to defeat Iradocc, but to rid Dark Magic of its existence."

Head lowered, Riley mumbled, "I want know more about what I'm supposed to do. I'm still lost and don't even know where to start. How does this Dark Magic have anything to do with me?" He took a breath. "Where did you go after that debacle with the stall-keeper? I tried coming with you, but . . . something happened. I lost sight of you and ended up having to hide from the guard, Edilie. My friend, Joseph, found me and I went with him to his and Kelvin—my other new friend's—hideout. By the way, who was that kid that the stall-keeper was being so mean to?"

"Tobias? He certainly appreciated you standing up for him. That is not common here. It used to be, but over time, things have taken a turn for the worse. I gave the lad a book as a gift for his brother instead of a slingshot and returned his money to him. Now, who are Kelvin and Joseph?"

"They're nice guys. Both of them were a little shocked that I had a star and that I wasn't from Leíso, but they got over that once we had a chance to get to know one another a little better. I plan on seeing them again, soon." Riley sighed. Caroline's words coming to him of wanting to return home because she felt uneasy about their being Leíso. He told Dorobonn these things, hoping the magician had some sort of advice to give.

"You should talk with your friend," Dorobonn said. "You must consider her choice and respect her decision. Did she explain to you why she felt uncomfortable?" His voice grew tight at that question.

"No, sir. I . . . didn't ask."

Dorobonn narrowed his eyes, which glinted. "When you return to the castle, ask her. If she wishes to go home, then take her back. That would not mean *you* need to leave. Just keep her out of harm's way."

"She told me she understood if I wanted to stay but she was ready to go home." Riley wished Caroline didn't want to leave, but so be it. He would talk to her later.

"That is fair. As I said, you must respect her decision, and then decide what you will do for yourself. Now, come with me, and we can start your training in the morning."

* * *

Dorobonn showed Riley a room where he could sleep for the night. The next morning, Riley woke up feeling more refreshed than he had in recent days. He went into the main room but Dorobonn wasn't there. A plate of bread, a red and yellow peach-like fruit, and a cup of water, awaited him. The fruit was sweet and savory. Inside Dorobonn's home—which Riley had not been able to get a good look at last night—was built of logs, presumably from the surrounding forest. Books lined the shelves and a stairway led to an upper floor. The main room was rather small, but quaint.

The fireplace to the side smelt faintly of ash from a fire the night before. Riley finished breakfast and went outside. The Endless Field was enormous. Riley couldn't see anything seemingly for miles, save the mountains where the storm cloud hovered—and even the mountains were specks in the distance. He thought he could make out a forest on the opposite side of the Endless Field but couldn't be sure.

"Wow!"

Dorobonn's home sat on the outskirts of the vast meadow. Riley admired the vastness of the field, wondering what lands lay beyond Zefa. "Good morning! I trust you slept well?" Dorobonn asked. He sat in a chair near the door with a book in his lap and gestured for Riley to sit in the chair next to him.

"Yes, I did. Thanks."

"Now, you have questions?" Dorobonn said, soon after Riley sat down.

"Yes. I don't understand what I'm supposed to do. You said I need to save Zefa *and* stop Iradocc. First off, what is Dark Magic? What will happen to my world if the Dark Magic takes over? I'm still having a hard time grasping this whole symbol deal." Riley touched his eye with his fingers, unconscious of the action.

Dorobonn leaned forward and propped his elbows on his

knees, his hands clutched together. A gleam of mystery came into his eyes. "First and foremost, it is understandable for you to feel this way. Nervous. I daresay you have no earthly idea where to start. Let me explain. The last two people of the star were unable to accomplish the prophecy. Yes, there is a prophecy. If neither the first nor the second could, then only one other can. But even then, the third person must defeat Iradocc once and for all. If he cannot, there is no hope. You are the third person, Riley. Only you can stop the Dark Magic.

"Now," he continued, "the Dark Magic is a treacherous power that spans as far back as Light Magic does. The two were created separately by opposing forces. Elomé, the One known to you as God in the Human World, is the ruler of Trinimea. Trinimea is a kingdom of indescribable beauty where life is eternal. No evil is allowed, nor anyone who practices Dark Magic. And then, there is Haedian. The Vile One rules that kingdom."

"Then who is Iradocc?" Riley interjected, promptly clamping his mouth shut in response to a stern side-eye from Dorobonn.

The corners of Dorobonn's mouth notched up. "As I was saying, Haedian is a kingdom of terror and pain. Demolics are those who have chosen to follow the Vile One. The Vile One is also the creator of Dark Magic. Dark Magic is a dangerous and sinister power. Light Magic was created by Elomé. It is a special gift and its most important purpose is to defy and overcome those that are in league with the dark powers."

Dorobonn turned to the cloud. "Dark Magic has its limits. If a Dark Magician uses his magic too much, it will eventually wear him down, drain him of his strength, leaving him vulnerable to attacks." Dorobonn pointed out the window to a cloud which loomed over Althia. "Do you see that Cloud?"

"Yes, sir."

"That Cloud covers the lands—kingdoms—which are being slowly enveloped by the Dark Magic."

"Will I need to help them as well?" Riley asked, as he feared the answer.

Dorobonn continued watching the cloud. "Yes. But not as of yet."

"I wanted to ask you. There's a voice I've been hearing lately. Well, kind of a voice. I've heard it a few times. It's . . . it gives me a sort of peace, in a way. I first heard it when I was at school."

"A voice, eh? And you say it give you a sort of peace?"

"Yes, sir. I can't explain it any better than that."

Dorobonn drummed his fingers slowly on the table. "There is no question, my boy, the voice that you are hearing is most certainly Elomé."

Riley's mouth parted, but no words came out.

"Indeed. Elomé 'speaks' to us in mysterious ways. Listen carefully, and store His words in your heart."

"I will," Riley insisted, still baffled over the idea that it was, indeed, Elomé speaking to him.

"Now, I overheard those creatures, who had harassed you yesterday, say something about you practicing magic. Is that true?"

"I haven't used any magic. Since I have a symbol, everyone's been accusing me of doing magic. But I found a book at Princess Lunaira's castle with magic words inside. I want to learn more! How can I learn the magic?"

Dorobonn inclined his head. "I will help you, but it will be difficult at first. You are yet a beginner." Then, seemingly pleased with Riley's eagerness, Dorobonn stood up from his chair and began walking towards the field. "Come. Tell me what you found in that book."

Chapter Thirteen

"So, the princess's steward informed you of a guest who was to come *when*, again?" Dorobonn asked. Matthew's claim seemed as much of a mystery to him as it did Riley.

"The day after Caroline and I came here. He didn't specify who the guest was. The weird thing is, he was . . . kind of freaking out when I asked about borrowing the book from the library. He said the guest has an interest in each and every tome."

Dorobonn contemplated this. "Interesting. If you happen to see this guest when you go back to the castle, report to me as quickly as you can. I wish to know who he is, myself." The tightness in Dorobonn's tone made Riley's stomach clench. He asked who Dorobonn thought it might be. The magician said he didn't know for sure and didn't want to make assumptions. "In the meantime, be on the lookout."

The sun shone bright as they trekked through the field.

"Éaltha," Dorobonn muttered, and a blue, filmy veil came out of the ground and created a dome over them. It rippled for a minute and then stilled. Riley wondered if it had disappeared.

"That is to shield us from any unwanted eyes. We will be invisible to those around us, but we can see them." Dorobonn touched the veil, and it rippled. Small, pale blue circles waved from his hand and faded like water. "When we use the magic, it will simply disappear into the veil."

Riley reached out and poked it with his forefinger. The veil felt similar to glass but softer. His finger couldn't push through the veil, but he could squish it. It wrapped around the tip of his finger. However, when he tried to pull his finger away, the veil refused to let go.

Riley tugged, but the veil would not budge. If anything, it grew tighter.

Dorobonn chuckled. "You must be firm with it, but not forceful."

Riley sighed and carefully pulled. Still, nothing happened. Riley pressed his other hand against the veil and yanked out of frustration.

"Ouch!" The joint in his finger popped. He stopped cold when the veil enclosed itself around his hand. *Good grief!* Riley's head drooped. "Umm, a little help?"

Dorobonn took Riley's wrist in his hand and gently pulled. The veil released him at last. Sheepish, Riley walked with Dorobonn to the other side and discreetly scowled at the veil, which sounded almost like it snickered at him.

Dorobonn stood beside Riley. "Now, we will start with gaphladeen. Remember, you must also learn that when your opponents are distracted, that is the perfect time to strike, but you must not allow yourself to lose focus, because you then become vulnerable."

He aimed his hand at the opposite side and said, "Gaphladeen!" A bolt of crimson lightning shot out of

Dorobonn's palm and struck the veil, soaking into it and causing a film of light red to bloom and then fade.

"Your turn."

Riley pursed his lips and said, "Gaphladeen!" Pinpricks lanced through his hand as though it had fallen asleep. Not painful, but not pleasant, either. He hadn't noticed the prickles when he'd tested out the magic yesterday. The lightning went a little off course but still hit the veil with satisfying potency. Red waves formed and then faded.

"It is unpleasant at first, but you will learn to overlook that," Dorobonn said.

Riley glanced at him.

"Now . . . palstona!" A bright, glittery, orange sphere formed, exploding into sparkles once it collided with the veil. "There are no unpleasant sensations with this one."

"I read about that one. It tickled. Palstona!"

Riley chuckled and caught Dorobonn smiling at him. "Do not touch the sphere, as it will most assuredly sting."

Riley laughed nervously. "Of course! No touching the sphere." He cleared his throat as Dorobonn eyed him suspiciously.

"Now, édian!" A patch of grass about three feet away from Dorobonn burst into purple flames.

"Édian!" Riley flinched at the small pinch in his fingers. A patch of grass close to Riley, kindled.

"You are a magic-trader, Riley," Dorobonn said. "Which means the powers you learn can be taught to others. In turn, others will teach you, as well. But you must be careful when it comes to magic-trading," he warned. "Magic-traders in the past have been tricked into learning Dark Magic, which became their ruin over time. If you are not confident in yourself, the magic will go awry and become difficult to control. You may even be tempted to give in to the Dark Magic as a way to cope."

How can I know when I see Dark Magic? Glazhier came to mind, but that didn't seem much different than Light Magic. "What kind of magician are you, Dorobonn? I thought I heard you're a Light Magician."

"Yes. I am a guardian of magic—a Light Magician. I teach Light Magic only to those who have been chosen for it. Dark Magic is learned and used out of a desire for power. Even Light Magic can be misused, with disastrous consequences." Dorobonn positioned Riley's arm. "Aim your hand straight ahead and shout the word, 'palstona.'"

"Palstona!" The glittery orange sphere of flame shot towards the horizon and then fizzled out when it hit the veil.

"Good. Now do the same with 'gaphladeen'."

"Gaphladeen!"

"Again."

"Gaphladeen!"

"Once more!"

"Gaphladeeeeen!" This power was more complicated for some reason, losing the route in which it headed both times. Riley narrowed his eyes and bit his lip every time the lightning angled in a different direction. Four times so far. Pinpricks made the experience even more unpleasant.

"Focus." Dorobonn came over and held his own hand out. "Gaphladeen." The crimson lightning shot forth.

Riley noted the hard look of concentration in Dorobonn's expression. He'd no doubt grown desensitized to the pinpricks.

"Palstona is easier to master. With gaphladeen you must be more attentive since it is stronger. Try it again."

Riley pursed his lips and focused on the horizon. "Gaphladeen." The lightning burst from his palm and hit the ground, creating a scorched spot.

Why can't I get this power down? He glared at his hand, breathing deeply. *I can do this. I can do this!*

"Gaphladeen!" The lightning began to head straight but then veered, flying into the ceiling of the veil. He grimaced at the pain in his palm.

"Riley, pay close attention to what you are doing. You may have never experienced an exercise this strenuous before, but it is necessary. If you are to fight this Dark Magic, you must know how to control the magic you are learning. This is what will help you to overcome Iradocc. These words are the most powerful you will learn."

Reminded of the battle, Riley's stomach roiled, and his mind moved at the pace of a snail. The sun beat down, only serving to tire him out more. Only a slight breeze helped to keep him more alert.

"Take a breather, Riley," Dorobonn instructed. "I want to talk to you about a few things."

Riley walked over to Dorobonn and sat on the ground with a sigh.

"You still have some time before the battle. Do not be discouraged if you do not perfect the magic right away. Rarely do we perfect anything we wish to master on the first few tries. I have no doubt that when the time comes, you will be prepared. As you may have discovered by now—life can throw things at you that you least expect, and very often, choices have to be made and action taken immediately. If I could, I would stave off the Vile One's storm and fight Iradocc myself to keep you out of this. Unfortunately, it cannot work that way." Dorobonn smiled at him and then gazed intently at the horizon.

Pointing at the mountains, he said, "Isleida." Some of the clouds over the mountains swirled and drifted nearer to their spot. Dorobonn slowly spun his finger in a circle and then spread open his palm. Something small and cold landed on Riley's nose. White, too.

A snowflake?

A light powdering of snow dusted the ground around them. The snow only landed where they sat. The rest of the field remained untouched, with the sun shining down on it as the snowflakes covered them.

Riley shivered, but not from cold—well, partly. He mainly shivered from excitement. "Is that magic I will learn too?"

"Aye. Someday, you will learn it. But not now. It is a more advanced magic that requires a great deal of willpower and self-control. There is much more magic for you to discover and learn, but that will be in the near future."

The snow ceased, and the cloud hovering above them dissipated. The only cloud within sight was the Vile One's path over the mountains. Even though it hadn't reached them yet, Riley fought the urge to back away from it.

"Due north."

"Hm?" Riley glanced at Dorobonn, confused.

"That is where the cloud is. Iradocc works day and night for the Vile One to bring about this world's ruin."

A flash of orange lightning lit up the cloud. Riley cringed. The power emanating from the Cloud intimidated him. Could that be the Dark Magic?

No. He prayed to Elomé for strength as fear and courage warred for space in his heart.

"Now, let us continue your practice." Dorobonn motioned for Riley to stand and follow him further into the field.

Riley worked on the "gaphladeen" word until the pinpricks in his hand numbed his skin. By the time late morning rolled around, Riley was already thoroughly exhausted.

"We will pause for today," Dorobonn said. "But tomorrow, we will continue into the evening." He grew silent for a moment. "Also, you need to take your friend, Caroline, back to the Human World, immediately. She is right in wanting to return. I sense something is wrong."

Riley opened his mouth, but Dorobonn raised a hand. "You must not allow your desire to practice get in the way of keeping her safe, child. Allow Elomé to guide you. Come to my cabin and rest for a moment, then you must hurry back."

Riley didn't want to stop, but he held his tongue. Dorobonn would say no. *How can I take a break when some monster is bent on destroying everyone in Leíso as well as myself?* He wanted to keep at it until he mastered the magic. He'd put his conversation with Caroline on the backburner for now.

Chapter Fourteen

Following a restful nap, a hearty lunch of bread, cheese, a couple of slices of salted ham, and water, Riley left the cabin. Dorobonn insisted he continue his practice on his own as well. He didn't specify *exactly when* to practice. Having decided to set aside his conversation with Caroline, Riley returned to his training. The forest would be a good place to practice, since he could use the trees and stones as targets.

"Palstona!" The sphere of glitter burst about halfway between Riley and the tree which stood twenty feet away. Why didn't it hit the tree? "Gaphladeen!" Same results. With a grumble, Riley shook out his hand. The pinpricks only made him more irritable.

"I *will* figure this out," he grumbled. He didn't want to think about what would happen if he didn't. Flexing his fingers, Riley lifted his face to the sky. Through the leaves he could see indigo clouds slowly moving in, as though observing him. He turned to the tree again. The last person he needed to have witness him do magic was Edilie. Riley had been out here for a good hour and a half practicing his magic but didn't seem to make any progress. Thunder sounded nearby. Perhaps he could wait out any oncoming storm and continue his practice afterward?

"So, how's the magic-boy doing?"

Riley paused and looked over his shoulder. Kelvin sat on a stump close by, watching him. Riley hadn't heard him walk up, so focused was he on his training. Riley glanced back at the tree, which seemed to mock him as it swayed placidly in the breeze.

"'Mind if we watch?" Kelvin asked.

"Sure!" Riley laughed, even though, in truth, he felt a little awkward with others observing him. *Maybe if I imagine it's Dorobonn watching me.* The idea gave him some comfort. He looked around. "Where's Joseph?"

"Right here!"

Riley almost jumped. He turned, seeing the vampire relaxing on the ground with his head against a stone, not far from where Kelvin sat. How did he get there so fast and without Riley hearing him?

Ah! Yes. He can transform into a bat. No wonder.

Shifting his attention to training, Riley agreed to having them watch. After all, he didn't believe these guys would criticize his efforts.

"Why do you need so much practice?" Kelvin asked.

Riley hesitated. If he told them the truth, they'd likely doubt him and he couldn't afford any more of that. He was refining his abilities. That would be a reasonable answer.

"I . . . I'm figuring out how to use this magic."

"What happens when you beat him? Iradocc, that is," Joseph asked.

"When," or "if"? "Well . . . I don't know. All the Dark Magic will be gone from Zefa. That much I can tell you." *Right?*

"What about for all of Leíso?" Joseph inquired, his brows slowly rising.

Ugh. Riley scratched the back of his neck. "I'm . . . hoping for that. Dorobonn said I would instrumental in keeping the Dark Magic from destroying the other kingdoms, too." He didn't know what else to say.

"I sure hope so!" Kelvin exclaimed as he knitted his fingers together behind his head and leaned against a higher section of the stump behind him. "I wouldn't want Ithara to be destroyed."

Riley glanced at him. "Is that where you're from?"

"Well . . . I've visited it many times. A nice little kingdom. The mizzers go there for their," Kelvin made air quotes, "'business.' Otherwise, it is an interesting place. I've never been inside the gates, but outside is pleasant."

"How come you've never been inside?" Riley questioned.

Kelvin shrugged. "I was told they don't accept mizzers."

"Huh." Riley couldn't imagine anyone turning away a nice guy like Kelvin. "What about you, Joe? Where are you from?"

The little vampire was fidgeting with one of his wings when Riley asked. Joseph's eyes were so intense with the task at hand, Riley almost decided to forget the question. "I'm from Lóthlar. That is where the Vampire Clan is."

"What's it like?" Riley asked, catching Joseph's abrupt pause.

The little vampire dismissively waved his hand. "It's a nice place." He then turned to the tree on which Riley trained. "Are you having some problems with your magic practice?"

Joseph's impassive reply in regards to his own home piqued Riley's curiosity. Of course, Riley didn't press him for questions, but he did want to know more about Lóthlar and why Joseph felt uncomfortable talking about it.

Riley gestured to the plant. "I've been having a tough time hitting that blasted tree!"

"Why?" Joseph asked, getting up. He stood next to Riley and stared down the tree, as if he could see something Riley couldn't. Joseph narrowed his eyes. He walked over to the tree and then glanced at Riley. He did a few takes before coming back. Riley lifted a brow.

"I was judging the distance from where you're standing in relation to the tree," Joseph explained. "You're not far from it. If you really focus on it, you should be able to hit it."

Riley rubbed his forehead. "I thought that's what I was doing." He then remembered Dorobonn's words to him. He needed to work harder on his concentration. Gaphladeen was not an easy magic to master. If Riley wanted to get better at controlling it, he couldn't allow his anxiety about improving quickly get the best of him.

I can't let my fears for my family or both worlds overwhelm me. Otherwise, I won't be able to do this. A louder rumble of thunder seemed to affirm his thoughts.

"Here. Use your magic, and I'll stop it. While it's stopped, we'll see where it's angling off." Joseph stood to the side.

Riley nodded. "Gaphladeen!"

About three feet away from the tree, the crimson lightning halted in its path. Riley turned, noticing Joseph staring hard at it, although the process appeared to strain him, for his body quivered while attempting to hold the lightning in place. Closing his eyes briefly, Joseph walked towards the lightning and observed it. Riley gradually extracted his hand from it, amazed that the lightning bolt didn't move. He came up beside Joseph. Riley could see individual sparks and faint electric waves emanating from the lightning. Joseph barred Riley from getting too close. "This is where I saw it start heading off in a different direction," the vampire said, pointing at the end, which edged off to the side of the tree. Riley almost couldn't see it, but upon closer observation, he was able to make out where the lightning got a little off target.

If I'm to fight Iradocc, I need to make sure I've got him fully in my line of target. Riley groaned. He peered at Joseph, who touched his temple and backed away, clearly in pain. Without warning, the lightning shot onward, colliding into a different tree.

"Whoa!" Riley exclaimed, a beat late.

"Sorry. My ability . . . it takes a lot out of me. I need to be careful when I use it." Joseph went to where Kelvin sat and leaned against the stump.

Riley and Kelvin watched Joseph, worried.

"Don't stress yourself out, buddy," Riley said. "I appreciate the help."

Poor little guy. *If Glazhier's after him, how could he fight?* Riley's thoughts were interrupted as a drop of rain landed on his hand. Riley looked at the clouds, and a droplet landed in his left eye. *Ow! Best go ahead and get as much practice as I can in.*

"'Buddy'?"

"Like 'dude,' it's the same thing as saying 'mate.'"

He needed to remind himself that many of the words he used were new to the people of this world. Riley took a deep breath and aimed once more at the tree. Concentrate. That's what he needed to do. Concentrate. "Palstona!"

Maybe? Maybe?! Nope.

The ball of glitter sped past the tree and into a different one. What was he doing wrong? Aggravated, Riley shouted, "Édian! Édian! *Édian*!" One tree, then two, then three burst with purple fire. It felt kind of good saying the word. Unfortunately, it also set ablaze a few trees, covering them in purple flames, and made his fingers a little sore. He grimaced at the sharp pinch which accompanied the magic, amplifying his frustration. "*Édian*! *Édian*!" Soon, the entire area lit up with a lavender/violet fire.

"Oh no!" Riley dared a peek behind him. Kelvin and Joseph gazed at the forest in amazement. Joseph got up and stared hard at each tree. The flames slowly disappeared. The trees were now blackened and burnt. Riley screwed his mouth to the side.

"Joseph. You okay?"

Riley looked over, seeing the vampire sitting on the stump where Kelvin had sat, holding his head, and gritting his teeth. "I'm fine," he groaned. "I'm fine."

Riley felt a stab of guilt. He'd caused the trees to catch on fire, and Joseph put out the flames, draining himself in the process. *What was I thinking?* "Sorry, Joe. That was stupid of me."

Joseph smiled weakly at him, only increasing Riley's guilt. Kelvin's hard gaze, on the other hand, served to make him feel worse.

At that moment, a flash of lightning enveloped the forest.

Not yet. Not yet! Riley protested. The sky darkened even more, defying his pleas.

"I'm gonna go back to the hideout. The storm shouldn't last long, but I'd rather not get drenched," Kelvin joked lightly. "Too bad the rain didn't start during your tantrum, eh, mate?" he said with a half-smile at Riley, who flushed, embarrassed. The forest turned a deeper green as the clouds blanketed what remained of the sun. Riley didn't want to stop. He couldn't stop. He needed this training. "Okay. You guys go on ahead. I'll come in a bit," he said, with an eye on the sky. Out of his periphery, Riley noticed Kelvin leaving. *I can't seem to figure that guy out.*

Assuming both had left, Riley murmured aloud, "I don't understand. Why is this so hard?"

"I wouldn't know."

Riley's heart leapt. "Joe! I thought you went back with Kelvin."

"Not yet. I need to rest my head." Joseph stared at the trees.

Why can't my problems do that? Burn away? Riley grunted, massaging his forehead.

"Sorry again for . . . you know." He couldn't help but feel like what he'd done was similar to Dorobonn's warning about using Dark Magic.

"It's fine. My head doesn't hurt anymore, at least. Why'd you set those trees on fire like that?" Joseph asked. "Doesn't seem like it helped you at all."

Riley sighed. What would've happened if Joseph hadn't stopped the flames from continuing? Would they have spread to the village? He didn't want to dwell on that possibility. A light sprinkle of rain pitter-pattered on to the ground. Riley's fingers stung and then buzzed—the aftermath of using magic for a good while, or so Dorobonn told him. He'd grow used to it the more he did it . . . or, so Dorobonn told him. Riley unconsciously touched his eye, hoping the star remained there.

"I . . . I don't know. Just irritated, is all."

Riley sat down on the opposite side of the stump and brushed his hand over his face. Why did he use the word to set the trees aflame? It was a way to release stress. He lacked confidence, and he knew that, ever since he'd arrived in Althia. No, before then! Ever since this blasted star came into the picture. *Be honest with yourself. For a while you've had confidence issues.* Riley remembered the first time he tried to stand up to Bryan in sixth grade.

Bryan had demanded Riley give him the answers for homework. Riley had refused, telling Bryan that they would get caught. Bryan insisted they wouldn't, but Riley angrily whispered, "If you can't figure out the answers on your own, then you might wanna start paying better attention in class!" He remembered the way Bryan's eyes had snapped. Riley's bravado failed him, and he'd tried to focus on his work.

A note slipped under his nose, with the threat, "*You have a death wish, don't you, kid?*" Riley had swallowed hard and couldn't focus on class for the remainder of the day.

Now Riley wondered what was going on in Bryan's life. What was his story? Did he hurt others as a way to cope with his own pain?

"I think I'll head back. You still good?" Joseph asked.

Right! Joseph was still there.

"Umm. Yeahhh, I'm coming, too." Riley got up and tottered a little bit as black specks filled his vision. *Whoa.*

"Are you okay?"

"Yeah, just got up too fast." Practicing magic took so much out of him. Riley looked at Joseph, hesitant. After causing Joseph to use his powers—thereby harming himself, he felt self-conscious about telling the vampire his troubles.

"You want to talk?" Joseph asked, unexpectedly. Was Riley that easy to read?

"Um . . ." Riley peered at his friend, whose eyes—so serious for a kid his age—somehow made Riley want to tell him everything. "I . . . I'm just . . . I . . ." Riley slapped his hand on a tree, aggravated. "I'm so frustrated right now! I don't know if I can save Zefa. I'm afraid I'll disappoint everyone. I'm scared of battling Iradocc! If I don't save Leíso, the Human World is no better off. I just don't know if I can do this!" he exclaimed, waving his hands frantically.

Joseph didn't react. He merely cocked a brow as if telling Riley to continue.

"Here's the thing. There are two guys in the Human World who've picked on me. Both for different reasons. One of them has been bullying me for the past few years. The other has just recently started."

"I see. These . . . *guys* have made you less confident in yourself," Joseph observed. "That's understandable. I struggle to focus when I remember Glazhier's oath to kill me."

Who wouldn't struggle with that? That's no different than Iradocc with me.

A drizzle came down on them, cleansing the forest with a fresh, spicy scent. The trickle of the river close by soothed Riley's senses. He wanted to take his mind off of his troubles for a moment. "So, this power you have. How have you managed to tame it?"

"It . . . I still have difficulties. When I discovered it, it didn't always work. It took me a long time to figure out the pattern. When I use my power in anger, there are huge consequences. For example, I intended to stop one of the other vampire boys from hurting a friend of mine's little brother. It worked, but I didn't know how to unfreeze him. No one knew it was me, and I never said anything. I got so scared. He unfroze about a day later, but I'm still not sure how that happened. Thankfully, ever since Kelvin and I met, we've become good friends, and it's nice having a friend I can trust. He says he wants to protect me from Glazhier. He must understand, though, that I don't want protection—not if it means putting friends lives in danger."

Riley glanced at Joseph. Something flashed in the vampire's eyes. Concern. Joseph stopped walking and faced him. "You must understand, Riley. I left my family in order to protect them."

Silence penetrated the air. His friend sat there silently, then turned away—mouth set in a firm line—and headed in the direction of the hideout. Riley gazed at the sky and then at Joseph. Riley shook his head, everything had become so complicated. The rainwater poured down, drenching him.

Addison Dixon

What is it you want me to do, Elomé?

Chapter Fifteen

Riley trudged through the village, not looking forward to the talk he'd have with Caroline. Okay, so he took a tad longer practicing than he should've. *But I needed to practice!* Riley reasoned with himself for the umpteenth time that day. *How else could I protect her if I don't?* A niggle in the back of his mind warned him otherwise. As foreboding thoughts filled Riley's mind, he broke into a sprint.

The rain stopped by the time he made it to the castle. Now the evening sun beat down on him, drying him quickly. Sweat trickled into his eyes, making them sting. He overheard villagers whispering, but paid them no heed—but perhaps he should have . . . Riley huffed as he climbed the castle stairs and slowly opened the door. Upon entering, he heard voices from within the library. Lunaira and Matthew's. Riley crept closer when he heard his name and the word "book."

"It is imperative. The book must be kept safe. If he takes it, it could be disastrous," Lunaira said.

"What do you propose we do, my lady?" Matthew

inquired. There seemed to be a hint of caution in his tone. "By the way, our guest wished me to inform you that he will be arriving late."

"I understand. He must have a good reason for being late. Remind me, Matthew, who is our guest?"

That caught Riley off guard. How could Lunaira forget who their guest was?

"Your highness, our guest is Sir Leod.

"Ah. Yes. I recall. Concerning the book—as I said earlier, I will take it with me."

"Take it with you?" Matthew repeated. "Won't that be risky?"

"It is what must be done," Lunaira answered. "I do not believe he can be trusted."

Who was she talking about, and what book? Riley could only assume she meant she was afraid of him taking the magic book she'd seen him read. Matthew must've told her about Riley's interest in borrowing it from the library. Not only that, but who was this Sir Leod? Chairs scraped against the floor suddenly, making Riley jump. He had questions, but knew it might be dangerous to ask. He went on to his room—only two doors down the hall—opened the door, and soundly shut it, acting as if all was natural. Lunaira and Matthew left the library, acting as normal as two humans who'd just been caught conspiring, could. Matthew gave Riley a nod but Lunaira eyed him questioningly. Did she suspect him of overhearing their conversation?

"Hi, Lunaira," Riley said, hoping the smile on his face appeared genuine.

"Riley," she answered with a short curtsy. She then paused. "Do you mind if I have a word with you?"

Despite knowing he had to talk to Caroline, Riley shrugged. "Sure! What's up?"

Lunaira swept her hand to the library. "In here, if you please?"

Hmm. Maybe she wanted to discuss matters about the book and their guest. Lunaira walked into the library, her silken green dress swishing gently with each step. Riley followed, wondering why the atmosphere felt tense. Lunaira sat down on a stool close to the magic book. Riley made a point not to look at it, as that might bring about an interrogation. He wondered if she purposely put herself close to it. If anything, he would let her know that he could wait to read it again after the guest—Sir Leod—left. That was reasonable, right? No matter how he tried to assure himself that everything was fine, sweat began to gather on the back of his neck. Lunaira motioned to the chair across from her for him to sit. "Now, Riley. I talked to Caroline earlier. She said she's not been feeling well lately."

This wasn't the direction Riley expected. His stomach turned sour as he remembered Dorobonn's admonishment. "Not feeling well? How so?"

"She feels lonely."

Lonely? Why? She had Lunaira for company.

When Riley remained silent, Lunaira stated, "That's why I have taken the initiative to be the friend she needs." Lunaira's words felt like a kick to the gut. *The* friend? Riley's confusion skyrocketed.

"Wait . . . but . . . sh-she and I are friends, too. I-I don't get what you mean." Riley's face buzzed at Lunaira's insinuation. She'd taken the initiative to be "the" friend Caroline needed. Was she implying that Riley hadn't been a good friend? She didn't even *know* Riley! Or Caroline either for that matter!

"She hasn't had anyone around to listen to her problems. She feels neglected, Riley." The accusation and pity in Lunaira's eyes and tone made Riley's heart skip a beat. The burn mark grew warm. He'd forgotten all about it! Forcing himself to ignore it, Riley clenched his fists.

"That's-that's not . . . that's . . ." Riley couldn't get the words past his tongue. His mouth had gone dry. "No. That's . . ." Why wouldn't the words come?! "I don't . . . I don't believe it. She's told me I've always been there for her. I know she can have more than one friend, of course, but that doesn't mean I haven't been there for her."

Lunaira's eyes hardened. "Whether you want to believe it or not, it is true, Riley. You haven't been here for her. Perhaps in the Human World it was different, but she has felt all but left alone since arriving here. How do you not see this?"

That's it! Riley stood up and headed for the door. "I have not neglected her, Lunaira. It's simply not true!"

He heard the sharp scrape of a chair. "Do not speak that way with me, Riley! Caroline is lonely and distressed."

Riley rolled his eyes and turned to Lunaira, who stared at him with intense anger. "Distressed"? What an exaggeration! As soon as he opened his mouth to retort—

"She's right, Riley."

His face numbed. Caroline brushed past him and walked over to Lunaira, her eyes sad. How long had she been listening? "You've been so intent on your 'mission' since we got here, that you seem to have forgotten I was even here. That YOU asked ME to come with you through the door to this new world. Lunaira's the only one who has given me some companionship since we have been at this castle!"

"I'll leave you two alone for a moment," Lunaira said.

Riley sighed inwardly in relief but couldn't understand Lunaira's accusation. "Lunaira said that you often feel lonely. Why is that?"

Caroline's expression stayed impassive. "Yes. I told her that.

She knows what it's like to be lonely, and so that's one way we can relate to each other."

Riley's brows furrowed.

"Oh, don't give me that look!" Caroline remarked. "Besides, you don't tell me everything that goes on with you."

"I—" He paused. "There's just a lot going on, Cara. I . . ." Riley hesitated. He felt something was off. Not with Caroline, but he sensed another ominous presence in the room, but they were alone . . . was it just his imagination? But if not, should he say anything more?

"Well?" Caroline demanded. Riley fought with himself to make eye contact with his friend. "I . . . I'm sorry, Cara, but there's so much going on. I can't tell you certain things for a reason."

Caroline's eyes reflected a sadness that twisted Riley's heart. It swiftly changed into anger. "I thought you were my friend?"

"What the—of course I am, Caroline! Besides, I don't think Lunaira trusts me." Riley now felt uncomfortable around the princess, wondering what she truly thought about him.

Caroline waved her hand dismissively. "She's royalty and has to deal with a lot of difficulties right now."

Riley bristled. "I get that. As I said before, I've had to concentrate on learning magic so that I can battle Iradocc, who is—I might add—trying to kill me."

Caroline snorted and said, "And might I add that Lunaira could be killed herself at a moment's notice by anyone. As a royal, her life is pretty much always in danger."

Riley gawked. He couldn't believe Caroline was downplaying his impending battle with Iradocc. Yes, he didn't doubt Lunaira had to watch her back at times, but Caroline acted as though his issues were nothing but a minor annoyance!

"The only reason Lunaira trusts you is because you have somehow earned her favor," Riley remarked. "Lunaira said that you are feeling lonely. I don't understand. There's no reason why you should feel lonely. I've been here all along." He regretted the statement as soon as he said it. Caroline's eyes snapped.

She jabbed her fingernail into his chest, making him wince. "It just shows how little you know about me! You've gone off without telling me anything that's going on! I've wanted to talk to you, but I barely see you anymore. I've dealt with loneliness for a while. Lunaira understands. She's been there. You wouldn't know because you grew up with siblings that you hung out with. I've always been overlooked." She paused as her chest rose and fell heavily. "If you're going to be so secretive and distrusting towards me, then obviously we aren't as close as I always thought that we were!"

Riley reeled back as if slapped. The pain of the burn mark increased.

"Don't do this, Caroline. I can't tell you because . . . because . . ."

"Because what? You don't trust me?" Caroline asked in such a point-blank manner, that Riley made longer eye contact than he'd meant.

"No . . . it's not that. It's just—I can't tell you." He despised keeping stuff from her, but if she knew what was happening, that her life could be in danger! *What am I talking about? She's already in danger!*

"Please, Caroline. You must understand. You . . . I . . . you're in danger. I'll . . . I'll take you back to the Human World, like you wanted!"

Caroline narrowed her eyes. "I'm in danger, alright. The Dark Magic. You're keeping things from me because of the Dark Magic! You're taken over by it. Otherwise, you wouldn't be keeping secrets from me. How do I even know you *would* take me back? You've been acting so strange lately."

Riley's entire body numbed. Could it be true? Had the Dark Magic begun influencing his thinking? No. Yet could that be the explanation for why he was struggling with his magic? He didn't want to believe this possibility.

She looked on the verge of tears. "I understand that you don't want me to worry, but I am worried. Do you think I can't handle anything?" She clenched her fists and backed away a few steps as if afraid of what Riley would do. She muttered, "I'm scared, Riley. I don't know what's going on. I don't know what to think."

The following sentence smote Riley.

"If you don't trust me, what good is our friendship?" After that, she said nothing else.

Riley didn't know what to think. A part of him felt angry. Fine! Let Caroline be that way. If she's too stubborn to listen, there's no point in explaining anything else. Nevertheless, Riley's heart sunk at Caroline's words. And he felt powerless to explain everything to her, not with the Vile One possibly listening. Was that the dark presence that he'd sensed earlier? A headache pounded at the back of his head.

The sound of a rustling dress caught his attention. Riley gritted his teeth. Lunaira stood in the doorway with a cold look in her eyes. How much did she hear? She quietly went over to Caroline and took her arm.

"Come on, Caroline. Let us go get some fresh air." She gently tugged Caroline along. Caroline didn't spare Riley a second glance. Once Caroline left the room, Lunaira came back in and put her hands on her hips. "I am trying to protect my people, Riley. I also wish to protect my friends."

Riley stared at Lunaira. Disbelief and fury warred within him.

"Lunaira, I can give her protection as well. I know Caroline." His eye contact with Lunaira wavered at his own words. Caroline claimed he didn't know her as well as he'd thought. Maybe she was right. But that didn't mean that their friendship wasn't true. He cared about her and would do his best to protect her! Dorobonn had admonished him, and he should've listened.

"How can you defend her and keep her from harm, Riley?" Lunaira demanded, "when you can't even protect yourself?"

What?! No. Lunaira was wrong. He'd show her! Running over to the bookshelf, Riley pulled the magic book out and slammed it on the table—grimacing at the loud *thunk!*—and flipped the pages.

"Riley, what are you doing?"

The shock in Lunaira's voice satisfied Riley, albeit a slight niggle of uncertainty entered his mind, alongside the adrenaline. What if Caroline was right about the Dark Magic thing? He waved the concern off.

"I'm going to show you that I can keep Caroline safe!" he remarked to Lunaira, without turning around.

The audible gasp from her, for some reason, made him falter—fighting between his desire to prove Lunaira wrong and worried that the Dark Magic claim was legitimate—but only for a minute. His heart thudded fast and eagerly. That had to be a good sign! This excitement. It must mean he was doing the right thing!

"Riley, don't do this. You don't know what'll happen if you . . ." She didn't continue, but her tone sounded almost desperate.

Riley's chest tightened. No. He wouldn't be afraid this time. Not this time! His arms shook, however, as he kept flipping the pages.

"Riley, if you do not cease this instant, I *will* have you arrested!" Lunaira's tone, so authoritative, froze Riley.

"A-arrested? For what?" He looked at her, stunned. She stared back, her expression cold. She even had her arm raised as if *she* would attack *him* with magic.

"What's the matter?" Riley didn't mean for his tone to sound challenging, but to Lunaira, that must've been how it sounded, for she jutted her chin out and said in a commanding voice,

"What's the matter? The matter is that you might destroy everyone and everything with your Dark Magic."

My Dark Magic?

"Why do you think I practice Dark Magic? I don't understand! What have I done to make you think that? You know about Light Magic, right? Dorobonn is training me in using Light Magic."

Lunaira replied, "Of course I am aware of Light Magic, Riley. But I've suspected you of practicing Dark Magic ever since you became interested in the book. It is a book of power."

"The magic I'm learning is Light Magic. I would never use Dark Magic. Hold on, is that why Matthew doesn't want me to read it? Because he—and you—are afraid of my misusing it?"

"It is a book of power," Lunaira repeated. "Meaning, it could easily fall into the wrong hands."

"And you consider *my* hands the wrong hands?"

He couldn't help but think Lunaira was hiding something. She gestured for Riley to leave the room as she, herself, headed for the door. "You should understand that Dark Magic isn't to be trifled with."

Just then, aggravation raced through Riley's veins. He picked out a word from the book—"*Táyathor* – to shield one from danger."

"I know Dark Magic isn't to be trifled with, Lunaira! You just have a hard time trusting anyone! You don't have the power to protect everyone. Táyathor!"

"Riley!!"

Panic speared Riley in the belly. Caroline's scream rang in his ears. Her tone sounded frightened. Shoving away from the table, Riley bolted for the hall—seeing no one.

No. No. No. The word couldn't have sent Caroline and Lunaira away. It clearly said, "to shield one from danger." He knew the girls hadn't left the castle—he would've heard the door open and shut. Riley dashed back to the book and feverishly reread the sentence. *"To shield one from danger."* Did that have some sort of hidden meaning? What if it meant to make that person *disappear* from the danger? He hadn't meant to do that! Was that why Lunaira had tried to warn him? He couldn't breathe. Couldn't breathe! "What have I done?" The whisper came out strangled. *Okay. Calm down. There has to be a reasonable explanation.* The thought did little to bring him comfort. Perhaps he'd been too wrapped up in his emotions that he didn't hear Caroline leaving the castle. That must've been it! As ridiculous as the assumption sounded even to Riley, he ran to the castle door and, with a grunt, pulled it open. He didn't see them anywhere.

"Is anything the matter, sir?" A guard walked up, eyeing Riley with a raised brow.

Riley, attempting to keep his composure, merely asked, "Did you happen to see the princess and Caroline walk out this door a moment ago?"

The guard shook his head. "No, sir."

This couldn't be. Had he sent them away with the magic? His face turned pale at the thought.

"Are you alright?" the guard asked but Riley couldn't hear him. His ears rang. Heading into the castle, Riley started to sway. This couldn't be happening. His eyes blurred. His mind went blank. Caroline and Lunaira had been right outside the library. *"You're keeping things from me because of the Dark*

Magic! You're taken over by it." He did it. They disappeared because of him. He'd been so willing to prove himself and it had done just the opposite. Leaning against the wall for support, Riley fought the urge to shout out his frustration. He pounded his fist to the wall and covered his eyes with his other hand. How—?

Just then, a malevolent chuckle from within the library made his skin crawl. Riley turned towards the room and slowly walked in. He searched the room with his eyes. The sinister feeling he'd had when talking to Caroline filled every corner of the library. He jumped when the door slammed shut. The candles blew out.

Of course.

The burn mark grew warm. Out of instinct, Riley glanced in the mirror. A dark figure appeared behind him.

Riley didn't dare look over his shoulder. The edge of a blade hovered only inches from Riley. He flinched, sucking in a sharp breath. "Who . . . who are you?"

The man whispered in his ear, making his hair stand on end. "I believe you know. I am Iradocc. I am the one who killed the People of the Symbol, and who is now coming for you."

This was Iradocc? Riley's heart jolted. Was Iradocc ready to battle him now? The idea made him sick.

"The frightened pounding of your heart delights me," Iradocc drawled. "I would very much like to end you here and now, but sadly, it is not yet time."

Despite that, Riley felt little comfort. This would only prolong his apprehension concerning his upcoming battle. "Why are you here?"

"Perhaps a bit of toying with my prey. One who is supposed to have such courage, but . . ."

Gulping, Riley touched his star, unconscious of the action. *He's right. My star is a symbol of courage. I need to show him*

I'm not afraid. Or at least act as if I'm not. This proved more difficult than Riley thought. He forced himself to turn around, and lifted his eyes. The person from his nightmare seemed to have manifested before him. Granted, Iradocc didn't have flames surrounding him this time, but the darkness somehow augmented the demolic's threatening appearance.

The sword traveled down to Riley heart.

"I have taken your friend and the princess to Elluciéna." Iradocc's face glowed in what little light shown through the window. His ice-blue eyes glinted. Somehow, his eyes were vaguely familiar, but why?

"Are you brave enough to attempt saving your friend? Do the princess and the young lady matter enough to you? What about your family? Your pathetic efforts could prove to be an amusing diversion."

Caroline and Princess Lunaira! My family! Riley backed up as the sword drew closer and closer to his chest. "I will save them. I will! I will prove that I can battle you." He grunted as his back made contact with the wall.

Iradocc's mouth contorted into a hideous grin. "I have your family and your friend. I also have the princess! It is only a matter of time before I eliminate *you* as well. And you will no longer be standing in my way."

Iradocc disappeared, but his voice echoed through the empty room.

Riley's body grew cold. Caroline *and* the princess had been kidnapped; and all because of Riley's irresponsible behavior! If only he had listened to Dorobonn. What had he done?!

Chapter Sixteen

Riley collapsed in a nearby chair.

My family?! What . . . Caroline and Lunaira . . .

The words spun around in his brain, his head ached.

"*. . . It is only a matter of time before I eliminate you as well . . .*" Iradocc's voice taunted. Riley leapt from the chair and ran for the door, swinging it open. He bit back a yelp, for Matthew stood at the doorway, with a slightly bored expression.

"Why, sir, whatever is the matter?" The steward peeked in the room as though expecting to see another person.

Riley opened his mouth but stopped himself. Should he tell Matthew about Iradocc?

"Iradocc was here. He took Lunaira and Caroline." Was it his imagination, or did Matthew's eyes gleam?

"He took them? Where?"

"E-E-Elluciéna."

"What? Iradocc kidnapped the princess? How?" Edilie exclaimed, appearing around the corner behind Riley.

"Yes. He just . . . showed up and then abducted her and Caroline."

Matthew narrowed his eyes. "That means . . . did you speak with him?"

"Yes, he told me he'd kidnapped them and that I must battle him to save them *and* my family." Short and sweet explanation. Hopefully, Matthew wouldn't question him further.

"Why did he kidnap them?"

"I . . ." Riley shook his head. "I don't know. I do know one thing. I have to go to Dorobonn with the magic book—"

To Riley's surprise, Matthew came within inches of him. The steward's eyes flashed with a strange light. "Why must you take the book? It is the property of the princess."

Riley glanced to the side. Why was Matthew acting so strange? He didn't even seem overly concerned that the princess had just been abducted! Matthew turned and whispered something to Edilie, who nodded and headed out the door.

"I'm aware of that. But it may have answers as to how the princess and Caroline could be set free!" Riley said. Best not to go too deep with the steward. Who knew what went through his mind? Matthew shook his head.

"I am sorry, Riley, but that cannot be allowed."

Since when did Matthew use Riley's name? "This conversation is getting us nowhere, and certainly not helping the princess and my friend!" Riley brushed past Matthew. His glare bore in Riley's back.

"Riley." Matthew sounded creepily calm. "For safety measures, it would be best if you remained within Zefa. This is for your own wellbeing. Considering that Iradocc is out there, it would be dangerous for you to be out wandering alone."

Stay in the village? Yeah, right! Wait. Why didn't Matthew question Iradocc's presence?

"No problem." Without another word and before Matthew could object, Riley left the castle and headed for the forest. The late evening sun pierced through the trees. Upon arriving at Tranien's Door, Riley grabbed the knob, hard. Whatever Iradocc had done to his family, he needed to see them. Now. When he opened the door, it was nighttime in the Human World. The moon brightened the forest and cast shadows everywhere.

Riley stiffened as he trod through the shadows. Shoving his hands in his pockets, he sought out the best way to explain to his family that had been happening. If there was Dark Magic here would his Light Magic be enough to save himself or them? Riley flinched at the shrill sound of a screech owl flying overhead.

"What're you doing out here, buddy-boy?"

Riley froze. Someone was here! Scrambling to the closest tree, Riley put his back to it, heart drumming. He slowly peered around the trunk. There was no one in sight. The voice had been low, but he thought he recognized the source.

"Why do *you* want to know?"

Okay, that was Bryan. Who and where was the first voice he'd heard?

"Uncle Les was asking. He told me to go find you." Felix! Riley recognized the cold, smug tone. Although, the voice sounded even more so since Riley's confrontation with him. He quietly lowered himself and crept over to a small clearing. There! He could see them both. Felix had one of Bryan's jacket lapels in his fist. What was Bryan doing out here? Riley couldn't quite see Bryan's face from where he hid. However, the moonlight shining on Felix's face clearly revealed his cruel nature. The night air was still, as though anticipating Felix's next move.

"I . . . was out because I felt like it." Bryan's hoarse voice reminded Riley just how skittish the guy was around his cousin.

"Is that so?" Felix sneered.

"Look, Felix, if Uncle Les is expecting me back, I'll go back. Just . . . just let me go, please." The nervousness in Bryan's tone made Riley pause. Here was a kid who acted tough, but deep down, he truly was scared. Riley's stomach tightened. He wanted to help, but what chance would he have against a big guy like Felix, who could, no doubt, take him out in a heartbeat!

"What's the matter, Brye? You okay?" Riley's ears rang, even though Felix wasn't threatening him. Bryan squirmed here and there, as he tried to pull himself out of Felix's grasp.

"Leave me alone, Felix," Bryan murmured.

Felix sniggered.

C'mon, Bryan. Just walk away from him.

"Now, why would I want to do that?" Felix replied, finally letting go of Bryan's jacket. He began to circle Bryan, like a wolf with its prey. Bryan's fingers stiffened, as if he were trying to decide whether or not to fight Felix. "You wanna take your chances against me, buddy-boy?" Felix said in a low voice, placing himself before Bryan. "You wouldn't last five minutes." Riley caught the venomous glint in Felix's eyes. Bryan wavered, even as he began to lift his fists. Felix smiled, challenging Bryan to throw the first punch. For a moment, Bryan actually seemed to consider it. Riley could feel the tension thickening between them.

"Go on. Do it," Felix spat.

In all his four years of knowing Bryan, Riley had never seen him so defeated. Bryan let his arms drop to his sides as he said,

"Sorry, Felix. Not this time."

Felix smirked. "That's what I thought! Too bad it doesn't matter what you say. I'm gonna some fun."

Sweat beaded Riley's forehead. *I have to do something!* "Palstona!"

The glittering ball smote Felix dead-on and he crashed to the ground. Bryan staggered back and then ran, not in the least bit hesitant. Felix got on all fours and shook his head. He wasn't as affected as Riley thought he'd be. "What the heck was that?!" he roared. Riley kept hidden, but Felix's voice drew nearer as he snarled, "whoever you are, I'm gonna kill you!"

Time to make a break for it! Riley bolted further into the forest, knowing that Felix could hear his footsteps. "Run all you want! You're as good as dead, anyway."

Felix's unnatural behavior at school came to mind, pushing Riley to run faster. Dark Magic. He recalled seeing, what he now believed to be Dark Magic, in Felix's eyes at school.

Riley looked over his shoulder, seeing Felix not terribly far behind. *How do I get away from him?!* "Whoa!" Riley tripped over a tree root and landed on his stomach. Winded, he peered up at the tree. That's it! He jumped, reaching for the closest branch.

"I know I heard you! Get back here, you little—!" Riley didn't hear the rest of the threat as he pulled himself up, clenching his teeth to keep from grunting, as he climbed onto another branch above him.

"Where'd you go?" Felix hissed, standing directly below the branch that Riley was crouched on.

Riley breathed as quietly as possible. His left leg began to cramp. Felix scoured the area, looking more like an animal than a human.

"When I find you, you're gonna wish that you hadn't done that." Felix made it sound as though he knew Riley was there. But how could he? Come to think of it, he hadn't even seemed surprised that what he'd been hit by was clearly some kind of magic. Felix seemed to eventually give up and disappeared deeper into the forest, muttering to himself. Riley decided to wait a few more minutes before climbing out of the tree, almost collapsing to his knees with his numb leg. Recalling what Dorobonn had said about Dark Magic in the Human World, Riley thought about Felix's behavior and then about his own family. What if they'd been affected like Felix had? He needed to hurry!

Chapter Seventeen

Riley scrambled up the hill to his house. It was still night, but Riley paid no mind to how much of a ruckus he created as he swung the door open and shouted, "Mom! Dad! Terry! Braydon!" The house was dim and quiet.

"Mom? Dad?"

Someone should be coming down the stairs or out of the living room by now. Instead, there was an eerie quiet. The wooden floor creaked as he stepped on it, but otherwise, the kitchen was dead silent.

"Terry? Braydon? Where are you guys?"

He crept halfway up the stairs, unnerved by the loud squeak of each step. No one said anything. No doors opened. The dark foyer offered no relief. Riley paused. He felt, for some reason, that he should check the living room. Riley held his breath. He placed his hands, a little unsteadily, on the doorframe to the living room and peered in.

"Mom! Dad! Terry! Braydon!" Riley's heart began to beat normally at the sight of his family. His parents sat on the couch while his brothers sat in chairs, side by side. They didn't turn to acknowledge him, however. Only their eyes moved. The stillness was deafening. Goosebumps spread up across his arms as his family's eyes turned to watch him. Judging by their expressions, it looked as if they'd been frozen.

"Mom. Dad. Can you hear me?"

Riley's heart plummeted when his mother's eyes welled up. At least they could hear him. They couldn't speak, though. They all looked at him in terror. No. That couldn't be. Riley knelt before his parents with tears forming in his own eyes.

"I wish you could tell me what happened. There's so much I want to say!"

Despite them not being able to talk, Riley so desperately needed to tell them what he'd been doing. It weighed on him so much, it seemed to crush his lungs. Taking a deep breath, Riley said, "I . . . this star. This star that everyone thought was a tattoo —it's not. It's actually a Symbol. One that is related to a prophesy from another world. I know this is sounding crazy, but I've been chosen to battle the Dark Magic that is destroying the world of Leíso, where the People of the Symbol once lived. They were killed hundreds of years ago by a demolic named Iradocc. He has discovered me and wants to kill me, just as he killed the others." Could this story sound any more ridiculous? Riley wouldn't believe it himself if he'd heard it.

Tears ran down his mother's face.

Riley cleared his throat, trying his best to keep control of his own emotions. "I've been learning Light Magic from a magician named Dorobonn. He's helping me. And . . ." How could he tell them about Caroline being kidnapped? "Caroline Fairburn . . . has been abducted by Iradocc. He took her and Princess Lunaira."

His parents' eyes shone a mixture of astonishment and sorrow. "I—we got into an argument. After that, Iradocc came out of nowhere and kidnapped them. I didn't mean for it to happen." Riley bowed his head.

"I see you have come to visit your family," a menacing voice said. "Good boy."

Riley's head jerked up. He stood slowly, his eyes searching the room. He recognized that voice, and it seemed, by his family's expressions, that they did, too. They stared behind him, at the living room doorway, in horror. Riley closed his eyes, bracing himself. He slowly turned to Iradocc and glared at him. "What have you done to my family?!" In spite of the dread rushing through his body, Riley refused to be intimidated by him.

Iradocc smiled, his eyes drifting lazily towards Riley's parents. "Sitting ducks. They are powerless to help you." The satisfaction in Iradocc's tone made Riley livid. "They will be unfrozen *only* if you defeat me, which, of course, is very unlikely."

"Release them!"

Riley lifted his hand, but Iradocc tutted, "Now, now, boy. You may want to reconsider such a rash move. If you use your magic on me, I will deflect it, and it will strike and harm—or kill—one of your family members." He sauntered into the room, scoffing at Riley's efforts to shield his family by blocking them with his body, arms outstretched.

"You absurd child. You cannot protect them. I am not here to kill *them,* anyway." The corners of Iradocc's mouth curled into a mirthless smile. "After all, your death is more important to me than wasting my time on your family." Iradocc unsheathed his blade and then pointed it at Riley's chest, hissing, "You and that magician, Dorobonn, are in the way of the Vile One's plan to dominate both worlds, and it will give me great pleasure to eliminate *you* from the face of the Human World AND Leíso." His eyes glittered like steel.

Iradocc motioned to the back door with his sword. "I suggest you do not disobey me. It would cost you greatly. Come along. If you do not follow me this instant, I will freeze you and send you *and* your family to Haedian where I will kill them before your very eyes."

Riley gasped, holding up his hands. "Okay, I'll come with you. Don't kill them!" He glanced at his family, desperately wishing that he could assure them that he would return as soon as he possibly could. He hoped they understood that.

Please protect them, Elomé.

Iradocc followed him out of the house, then came to an abrupt halt. The moon's light shone on them, drenching the world in silver. "Our battle draws nigh, boy. Yet, there is one way, that if you so choose, you can avoid this war and save your family here and now.

You *are* aware that your symbol can disappear if you neglect it?"

Riley jerked a nod.

"Good. I will make you an offer—I allow you to stay here in the Human World, out of my way. You and your family live in peace. Your star disappears.

That symbol has given you much trouble, is that not true?" he said.

"I . . . yeah."

"If you choose to return to Leíso, I will have no choice but to kill you. If that happens, you will never see your family again. Is that what you want?"

Riley's blood iced over. "No," he muttered.

"I did not think so. If you return to Leíso and battle me and die, your family will stay frozen like this. Forever. What loving son would do such a thing? Therefore, why not remain in the Human World where you belong? Think about it. That star has caused you pain. Why suffer it?"

The offer was tempting! Riley, with all his being, wanted his family to be safe and he surely did not want to battle Iradocc. He knew in his heart, though, that he couldn't choose that path. What about Caroline? She would be trapped in Leíso! Would the Dark Magic disappear, or would it eventually take over the Human World? Also, did he *truly* want to get rid of his star? It had caused a lot of trouble, but it had done much good, in spite of that. And besides, Riley knew that it would be foolish to trust Iradocc's words. He had no choice but to continue.

"I *will* come back. I know you're lying." From what Riley had heard and seen of Iradocc, the demolic wouldn't be content with letting Riley continue to live. Not even in the Human World.

Iradocc's eyes flashed. "Foolish, foolish child. Your audacity will be your undoing."

In a swirl of dark mist, Iradocc disappeared, leaving Riley alone in the growing chill of the night.

Chapter Eighteen

The heaviness of Dark Magic lingered long after Iradocc vanished. Riley stole a glimpse through the window of his family's living room.

"*Your family will be fine. You must go now,*" said a warm voice. Dorobonn had said that the voice Riley heard was Elomé. It brought him peace unlike anything else in his life. Taking one last look at his family, Riley headed down the hill into the forest towards the door. The moon provided shadowed light for him as he tread carefully, catching himself any time he slipped. Upon arriving at the door, a strange and menacing voice whispered something in his ear, but he could not understand the words. Riley reached for the knob, not noticing the black mist swirling behind him. It slithered to the ground, up the door and on to the knob. Riley yanked his hand back. He kept his distance as the mist revealed a cloaked figure with loathsome orange eyes. The narrow pupils resembled those of a snake. The figure smiled, chilling Riley's blood. Sharp teeth–like a wolf's–shone in the moonlight.

"Who are you?" Riley stammered.

The figure revealed arms, thin and sickly. Sharp claws, or nails, protruded from his fingers.

"I have gone by many names. You know me as the Vile One."

"The Vile One?" Riley squeezed his eyes shut at the potency of the Dark Magic which emanated from this monster.

"Indeed." The Vile One turned towards the door. He then leered back at Riley. "Work for me. If you do, I promise you great power and wealth—more than your inadequate human mind can comprehend. Do you suppose I give this offer to simply anyone? You are the first Human from your world to have an accursed symbol. If you choose to work for me, you will be free of the pain that star has caused you. You will be stronger than any other human. If you refuse, Iradocc *will* destroy you."

Riley's heart hammered.

The Vile One's chuckle grew more maniacal. "I sense your fear, boy. Your heart betrays you."

He narrowed his eyes at Riley's heart. The burn mark. Riley covered it with his hand and shouted, "gaphladeen!" Why he used that word when he hadn't even mastered it yet, he didn't know, but apparently it was not a wise move. The devil collected the lightning into his gaunt hand and squeezed it in his fist.

What in the heck was I thinking?! Riley stared as the Vile One squeezed the magic into grey dust and threw it into the air.

"*That* is why you cannot fight me," the Vile One drawled. "Such a simple, silly, little child. I've wasted enough time with you as it is. Go play now. I shan't warn you again."

"No."

"You don't value your life?"

"I value others' lives more than I value mine. I *will* go back to Leíso, no matter what you say. You won't stop me."

"So be it." His voice rose. "You shall wish that you had

never returned to Leíso. You shall beg for mercy from the powers of darkness, and you shall receive none!"

The Vile One disappeared, as if he'd never been.

Slowly, Riley reached for the doorknob. He faltered as the Vile One's words echoed in his mind.

Riley feared he wouldn't be able to overthrow Iradocc, after all. The Dark Magic might be too strong.

"*You shall wish that you never returned to Leíso.*"

Riley leaned against the door and stared at the sky. "Am I strong enough? Everyone will die because of me, won't they? I'm not anywhere near Iradocc's level when it comes to magic powers. He'll kill me in battle or the Dark Magic will somehow destroy everything and everyone here. If he's anything like the Vile One, then there's no use."

A light breeze touched his cheek, reminding him of the tear streaks from earlier, for his skin was cold as the wind stroked it.

"*I am with you. You will be strong enough. Do not despair.*"

Riley unconsciously touched his star. "Help me to trust you more, Elomé."

Looking towards the door once again, Riley spoke aloud, "I . . . I *will* do this."

Chapter Nineteen

Riley dragged himself to the castle, exhausted. He needed sleep. Unaware of the sidelong looks villagers gave him, he entered the castle, not caring if Matthew was there or not. Fortunately, the steward was nowhere in sight. Riley went into his room and locked the door. He dropped on to his bed, and immediately fell into a dreamless slumber.

* * *

"Ah. So, you're the one I've heard about."

Standing in the forest—which glowed with a strange light—Riley looked over his shoulder. The voice seemed as if it came from behind him, but no one was there.

It sounded regal . . . cunning. Who in the world—?

"You are the lad with the star. Curious how a Human Worlder has been able to attain such a special and powerful gift." The voice now resounded everywhere around him. "I am anticipating our meeting."

"Who are you?" Riley asked, eyeing his surroundings, wary of anyone jumping out at him. "How do you know me?"

The voice laughed mockingly. "That shall be revealed soon enough."

* * *

Thunderclaps in the distance woke him up. It was afternoon. Riley rubbed his eyes, groggy but unable to sleep any longer. He looked out the window and saw lightning striking the tops of the mountains. He lifted the sash, and climbed down the tree just outside his window. This way, he wouldn't have to worry about the guards interrogating him. Particularly, Edilie.

Villagers were out and about, but many we're packing up items from their stalls and preparing to get inside their houses due to the rising winds. Something about this storm made Riley realize that it wasn't a typical storm. There was an unearthly feel in the air. The clouds were darker than usual. The lightning took the form of a jagged knife. A knife striking the very heart of the mountains. Riley unconsciously touched his burn mark over his own heart.

"Riley?"

Tobias lounged in a tree not far from the castle grounds.

"Oh, hi, Tobias!" Riley exclaimed. "What's up?"

Tobias clutched the branch he sat upon, maneuvered his body into a crouching position, and then slipped off the branch. He swung down, dropping to the ground. He scampered over to Riley, smiling. "Dorobonn's waiting for you at his cabin."

Riley lifted his eyes to the tree. "Is that why you were up there? Were you waiting for me?"

Tobias jerked a nod. "Yes! By the way, I wanted to thank you for helping me with that stall-keeper. He despises forest people. At least, that's what he calls us."

Riley grunted. He didn't feel like he'd helped much. After all, the crowd just about arrested him, and who knew what they would've done to Tobias? If anything, Dorobonn was the true hero.

"You're welcome." Guilt pricking him, he left it at that. When they arrived at Dorobonn's cabin, they spotted him outside reading a book.

"Dorobonn, look who I found!" Tobias exclaimed, waving a skinny arm. Dorobonn lifted his head and smiled.

"Riley, my boy! I am glad you were able to come. It is very nice to see you again."

"The Vile One has appeared to me, Dorobonn! I also saw Iradocc. He froze my family and tried to convince me to work for the Vile One. I said no."

Dorobonn grasped Riley by the shoulders. "Good! Now, you say Iradocc froze them?"

"Yes! They're not hurt, but they can't move."

Releasing Riley's shoulders, Dorobonn looked up at the sky. "It was a trap. He lured you to the Human World and used your family as a means to frighten you."

Thunder suddenly rumbled overhead. "Come," Dorobonn said. "Let us go inside. The storm will be upon us soon."

As they entered the cabin, Dorobonn passed his hand over each window, and as he did so a dark shade slowly lowered. Dorobonn drew up two chairs for Riley and Tobias. Wind buffeted the cabin, creating all sorts of creaking noises. Dorobonn lit several candles and placed them on the table and on the bookshelf. Riley wondered if the storm had anything to do with Dark Magic or if it was just a typical storm. After sitting down, Dorobonn paused a moment before continuing, "I haven't told you this, but Iradocc and I battled each other in L'Za. I traveled there as fast as I could but was too late. Iradocc attempted to convince me to work for the

Vile One as we fought. He threatened to kill me if I didn't join him."

A loud peal of thunder shook the cabin. Riley glanced nervously at the walls and windows. The candlelight sputtered but continued burning.

"You . . . you battled Iradocc?" Riley said quietly.

"Yes." Dorobonn's eyes softened. "I am glad you refused as well because if you had agreed to join the Vile One (out of fear, of course), he would've had you destroy Althia and you would never have seen your family again in the Human World, for the Dark Magic would have spread far and wide, unchecked. You have a strong heart, Riley. Weaker minds have fallen for Iradocc's words and paid the consequences. *Severe* consequences."

By now the storm had abated and they went outside. The air, clean from the rain, refreshed Riley. The clouds had departed—all except the One Cloud. "Why does the Vile One use a cloud, Dorobonn?"

"Storm clouds tend to strike apprehension into peoples' hearts. They are often seen as omens for bad weather which, as you know, can wreak havoc."

Riley hadn't thought of that. "I almost forgot to mention." He pulled down the collar of his shirt and exposed the burn mark. "I got this when Iradocc visited me in a nightmare."

Dorobonn's eyes flashed. "It's just as I feared. You have one, too. The burn mark is a sign of Iradocc's hatred. It is a personal reminder that he has a score to settle with you. It can only heal by means of forgiveness."

"Forgiveness from who? And how do you know so much about the burn mark?" Riley questioned.

Dorobonn pulled down the collar of his own shirt. His burn mark looked exactly like Riley's. "The one who receives the burn mark must forgive the one who inflicted it upon them. Iradocc gave me this one years ago."

Riley contemplated this. "I guess you haven't forgiven Iradocc yet? And why does he despise *you* so much?" He didn't like the idea of having to forgive Iradocc for giving him this burn mark.

Dorobonn didn't answer right away. He seemed to have something on his mind, for he turned his head from one side to the other, as if worried someone was listening and then said, "Iradocc and I have . . . a complicated history. We were friends in our youth, but he was abused by his family and, over time, became interested in Dark Magic. He wanted me to join him, but I had no desire to do so. This angered him and we parted ways. When we grew older, he confronted me—like he did you—in a dream. By then, I'd already been practicing Light Magic. It was there, in the dream, where I received a burn mark. A cicatrix, as it's called. A blemish. As for your question about forgiving him, I already have—in my heart, but I have not yet had the opportunity to tell him. It can only be healed if you acknowledge your forgiveness to the offender personally."

Riley glanced down at his own burn mark and then at Dorobonn's. Something bothered him about Dorobonn's story. "You and Iradocc were friends?"

"Aye. You must understand, Riley, Iradocc wasn't always the monster you know now. Unfortunately, familial circumstances and working for the Vile One has turned him destructive and hateful."

It seemed hard to believe, and yet Riley could tell Dorobonn was being quite serious. He just couldn't imagine the horrible individual he'd met was, at one time, a decent person. Riley thought about Bryan and his cousin. Riley didn't know much about Bryan's situation but he knew Bryan didn't have a great family life.

"Now that the storm has subsided, let's do a bit more training while there is still some light outside," Dorobonn said. Tobias excused himself to go home. The sky glowed pink and orange through the clouds, which slowly dissipated. Riley struggled to focus on his training, for Dorobonn's story and the cicatrix occupied his thoughts. If he wanted to defeat Iradocc and rescue his family, Caroline, and everyone else, he would need to get more serious in his training. He would think about everything else later. Needless to say, he didn't feel comfortable with telling Dorobonn about Caroline and the princess being kidnapped. Not just yet.

* * *

Several days passed and Riley found it harder and harder to focus. His nerves were so frazzled, he became moody and didn't want to practice. No matter what, though, Dorobonn kept pushing him. Riley knew there was still so much he needed to learn from the Book. One evening, after his training with Dorobonn, Riley made his way towards the Castle Library.

"You there! Where have you been?" Edilie demanded.

What does it matter? Riley wanted to ask. Best not provoke any of the guards however, particularly this one, if it could be helped. "I'm . . . I've been with my mentor."

Edilie sneered. "That magician fellow I've seen you with? Dangerous business to be with someone like him."

Why would it be dangerous? "Uhh, yeah. Look, Edilie, I need to g—"

"Matthew said that if anyone travels outside of the village, they are to be arrested." The smile curling his lips chilled Riley's heart. "Do you know what that means?"

Riley sidled away, believing he knew full well what Edilie

insinuated. The guard would use any excuse to arrest him. "Hold on, Edilie. When did Matthew say that?"

"After you told him about her majesty and the young lady's kidnapping. He made it clear than anyone who leaves Zefa is to be put in prison."

Edilie grabbed Riley by the arm.

"Wait!" Riley exclaimed. "You can't arrest me."

The guard frowned. "Why not?"

"Because if you do, then I won't be able to fight Iradocc! It's important that I do, Edilie. You can tell Matthew that if you want."

Edilie's scowl deepened. "To be sure, I *will*." He marched off.

Riley resumed his aim for the library. He approached it, feeling like he was being watched. Matthew was nowhere in sight, thank goodness. Riley grabbed the knob but the door wouldn't budge. *What?* He yanked harder, with no result. *Great. Matthew must've locked it.* Aggravated, Riley decided it best to just turn in for the night. The next morning, he walked through the forest, hoping for a bit of calm before training. As he walked, Riley felt, yet again, like someone was watching him. He scanned the forest but didn't see anyone. The hair on the back of his neck prickled. He breathed inaudibly, listening for any sounds.

"Hey, kid."

Riley's heart leapt into his throat. He turned around and spotted someone leaning against a boulder. He wore a hat, similar to Kelvin's. He also had on black breeches, a tan vest, and a white shirt. A mizzer? It had to be! How long had he been watching Riley? Why was he addressing Riley in the first place?

Chapter Twenty

Riley stared at the mizzer, unsure of what to do. "Umm. Who're you?" The mizzer didn't move an inch. His skin was a dark olive color and his eyes, deep green. Riley's blood rang in his ears. What did this guy want?

"So, kid, whatcha doin' out here, all by yourself?"

"Err . . . I'm . . . I was visiting a friend."

The mizzer sneered. "A friend, huh?" He pointed at Riley. "You're the magic kid with the star, arentcha? I've heard of ya." He pushed away from the boulder and sauntered over. Riley broke out in a cold sweat.

"You're Kelvin's friend."

Riley gasped. How would this mizzer know he was friends with Kelvin?

"I've seen you boys around. My name's Solben. I used to work with Kelvin. He's a good kid." Riley detected a note of sarcasm in that statement. He didn't quite know how to respond and backed off a few steps.

The mizzer folded his arms. "So, how's Kelvin-boy doing?" Solben asked, with a cold look on his face.

"He . . ." Riley cleared his throat and shrugged. "He's doing fine."

Solben narrowed his eyes at him. "What's wrong, kid? You're as pale as a ghost." Riley glanced to the side, wondering if he could escape and outrun this guy.

"I . . . I just need to . . . I need to head back to the castle."

The mizzer blocked his path. "So. Where's Kelvin?"

Riley hadn't expected that question. What would happen if he gave his friend's hideout away? "I . . . I don't know. I haven't seen him lately."

Solben narrowed his eyes at Riley. "Liar." Riley's stomach grew cold. "You do know. I saw you with him and that little vampire fella yesterday."

"What does it matter to you?" Riley said, trying sounding brave, although he wasn't feeling it!

"Watch your tone, boy," Solben snapped. "Kelvin's gonna come back with us. The gang has some . . . unfinished business with the kid."

"I'm not telling you where Kelvin is. Go away." Why couldn't this mizzer just leave him alone?

Solben's brows furrowed. "I see you're a loyal one. If you think you know Kelvin, you're wrong. He'll betray your friendship the first chance he gets. He's a loner. We took him in 'cause he didn't have a family. *We're* like family to him. He was selfish to run away."

"*You're* lying," Riley said. "Kelvin would never betray anyone! At least, not his friends. He ran away because you abused him. He doesn't want anything to do with you."

Solben stiffened, taken aback that Riley had the gall to stand up to him.

"You've got attitude, boy," Solben spat. "Kelvin's ungrateful to think that way of us. He's always been rebellious! As for *you* —you'll regret telling me that I'm a liar." He lunged for Riley.

Riley side-stepped Solben and ran to the other side of the boulder. The uneven surface enabled him to get a good foothold in order to start climbing. Eventually, he reached the top, rolled on to his belly and laid flat, hoping to hide himself from Solben.

"Where'd you go?" the mizzer exclaimed. Riley kept as silent as a mouse. He watched as Solben circled the boulder, while staying as close to the rock as possible.

"You blasted little—"

Unfortunately, Riley sneezed before he could muffle the sound. Solben immediately spun around and spotted Riley, who jerked back from the edge.

"Ha! You think that rock will save you?" Solben scorned. Panicking, Riley looked around. Maybe he could climb down the boulder and make a break for it. A hand snatched his collar and yanked him backwards. How did Solben get up here so fast?

"Gotcha!"

Riley fell hard on his back, knocking the breath from his lungs. Solben pinned him to the boulder, pressing into Riley's windpipe. Any effort to push Solben off was futile. "Now, be a good boy and tell me where Kelvin is. If you behave, I'll spare you."

Riley shook his head, struggling to breathe as Solben pushed his thumbs deeper into Riley's windpipe. He wouldn't betray Kelvin, he wouldn't! Riley could feel himself beginning to black out. Solben pressed one of his knees into Riley's stomach. "You're only making this harder for yourself, kid. You're not strong enough." Bryan's words from school echoed in Riley's mind, "You're not brave enough!"

Angling his hand at Solben, Riley croaked, "Palstona!"

The sphere hit Solben dead-on, who nearly fell over the side of the boulder, but caught the edge in time. Riley sat up and coughed as he rubbed his throat. He peered over the edge, seeing Solben release his grip and drop to the ground. The mizzer glowered at him. "You—"

"Solben!"

Kelvin's voice carried through the forest. Riley quickly glanced in that direction and saw Kelvin running towards them. A lower rumble of thunder startled Riley. It sounded like a warning. Kelvin stopped abruptly a few feet from where Solben stood.

"Solben, what's going on?" Kelvin demanded.

Solben narrowed his eyes. "None of your business, Kelvin-boy. Come to check on your little friend?" He glanced up at Riley.

Kelvin's gaze hardened. "I was nearby and overheard you."

"Oh, really? Nosy as ever, I see. If you must know, I'm busy dealing with your magician friend here. Then I was gonna come searching for *you*." He poked Kelvin in the chest with his forefinger. "It's about time you returned to the Mizzer Gang. Marcus isn't happy with you."

As they talked, Riley climbed down. Once he was safely on the ground, footsteps behind him stole his attention and he nearly yelped upon seeing Joseph standing there.

"I saw two other mizzers coming," Joseph whispered. "We need to get outta here." Riley turned to Kelvin, who was in the midst of a heated argument with Solben.

"I'm not going back. As a matter of fact, Marcus isn't my leader anymore." Kelvin swept his hand towards Riley and Joseph, stating, "Those—guys are like family to me. I'd rather go with them any day than with you mizzers." A flash of lightning lit up the forest, followed by a loud crack of thunder, as though backing up Kelvin's words. A small chirp sounded above them. Riley lifted his head, spotting the same golden-green bird that he and Caroline had seen upon their arrival in Leíso, perched on a branch. It observed him for a moment with its dark marble eyes before flying away.

"'Guys'? What does that word mean?"

"It's a Human Worlder word," Kelvin said confidently, if a bit defiantly.

"You found him!"

Riley, Kelvin, and Joseph turned around. Another mizzer—a bigger one—sauntered up to them with a contemptuous smile. Now how would they get away? He wore dark brown pants, tan moccasins, a black vest, and a faded white shirt. His hair came down to the base of his neck. The tip of his brown cap shadowed his eyes.

"Hey, Kelvin-boy. Who're these fellas? Your new friends or somethin'?" he said with a malicious glint in his eyes.

Kelvin looked at him angrily.

"Yeah, they're my friends. You leave 'em alone, got it, Gaith?"

The mizzer, Gaith, brushed his nose with his knuckle. "Still as rebellious as ever. Guess this kid needs some reforming, eh, Solben?"

"Heh, no question about it! Where were you, by the way? I've been waiting." Solben pointed at Riley. "That one has been causing problems, according to rumors. He's the boy who can do magic. The kid with the star. We've also got the vampire here."

Gaith squinted at Riley. Eyes widening, he let out an impressed whistle. "So it is. Well, well, well. And that vampire. He's the one Glazhier's after, isn't he? By the way, Marcus has been ranting about Kelvin-boy's behavior. The kid's in huge trouble." Gaith punched his fist into his palm. "Whattaya think, Solben? Take all three of 'em on?"

Riley didn't like the grin on Solben's face. "Yeah."

"*No*!" Kelvin protested. "You're not gonna hurt these guys! I'm not coming back with you and that's final! Marcus doesn't tell me what to do anymore."

Gaith rolled his eyes. "Pfft! As if *you* have any say in what Marcus can or can't do. Tell you what. Either you come with us, or your friends get it—starting with the vampire boy." Gaith made for Joseph, but Kelvin jumped in the way.

"Fine! I'll go with you. Leave my friends out of this." Solben and Gaith nodded to each other as if they'd planned this all along. Solben seized Kelvin's arms from behind. Riley paled. What were they doing? He started to say something, but Gaith held up his hand.

"Unless you wanna be taken in, too, I suggest you pipe down."

Riley wanted to protest, but Kelvin subtly shook his head.

He's trying to protect us.

"You've always been a rebel," Solben hissed in Kelvin's ear. "Brace yourself, kid. This'll hurt *you* more than it'll hurt *us*!"

Right after Solben finished speaking, Gaith delivered a sucker punch into Kelvin's stomach.

Kelvin doubled over, breathless. Following a second blow to the gut and then a punch to the eye, Solben pushed the young mizzer to the ground. Riley wanted to turn away, but his eyes were glued to the scene.

Help him! Furious and disgusted, Riley aimed a hand at the mizzers.

"Stop hurting him!" Riley cried. Solben and Gaith suddenly stopped moving.

"Wha—? What's happening?" Gaith demanded angrily. He shot a furious glare at Riley. "Are *you* doing this?! You better let us go if you know what's good for you!" Riley knew

Joseph had actually frozen them, but he wouldn't reveal his friend's ability.

"Riley . . . Joseph . . . don't!"

Kelvin gritted his teeth. As he struggled to stand, Riley took a step towards him, but Gaith stood in the way.

"Don't . . . don't fight 'em," Kelvin muttered.

"But–but, Kelvin . . ."

"Don't—fight 'em."

Riley's burn mark stung. He placed a hand to it. He couldn't just stand there and watch Kelvin get beaten up!

"That's right, boys," Solben gloated. "Kelvin's got some *stuff* coming 'is way and if you're smart, you won't interfere." Riley lifted his eyes up. Thunder shook the air and lightning split the sky. Foreboding penetrated the atmosphere and clutched at Riley's heart with an icy grasp.

Dark Magic?

"C'mon, boy. Marcus is waiting." Solben grabbed Kelvin by the scruff and pulled him up. Accepting his fate, Kelvin allowed himself to be forced along, like a dog on a leash. Gaith took up the rear. He whirled on Riley and Joseph and stabbed a finger at them.

"Final warning—stay out of our way! Otherwise, you'll get what Kelvin here got. Or worse."

Riley's stomach grew queasy at seeing Kelvin—so tough and strong-willed—beaten and bruised. Riley had never felt so helpless. Not since back in the Human World. Something pricked his eye. Riley rubbed at it but found nothing there. A loud peel of thunder rang in his ears. As he watched the mizzers leave, he had a strange vision. Riley saw Max, instead of Kelvin, and Bryan's gang, instead of the mizzers. When he gave his head a slight jerk, the vision dissipated.

Joseph hadn't said a word. His eyes never broke away from

the mizzers, even when they were out of sight. Eventually, he murmured, "We need to help him."

Riley agreed, but what could *they* do? "Yeah . . . but they might have Kelvin under lock and key. How're we going to free him?" The moment he said that, a bird chirped next to him. It was the golden-green bird. It tilted its head at him and let off a series of chirps. It then pointed its beak in the direction the mizzers had gone and then at Riley and Joseph. It repeated this a few times before flitting off. Was it trying to tell them something?

Wait. *Is it saying to go after Kelvin?* It couldn't be possible. Could it? He peered at Joseph. Solben had said that they would receive a beating like Kelvin if they followed. The bird appeared again. This time, further in the direction of the mizzers and chirped again. A second time, it looked at Riley, Joseph, and then towards where the mizzers had taken Kelvin.

"Is that bird talking to us?"

Evidently, Joseph had wondered the same thing as Riley. How could it be possible that a bird was able to communicate with them? Regardless, it was clear that he was, and that they were to follow. Joseph and Riley set off at a fast pace, determination in their eyes.

Hopefully they would get to Kelvin before those mizzers did anything worse to him.

Chapter Twenty-One

A light sprinkle of rain began to fall, but not enough to hinder them. The bird continued flying to and fro from branch to branch, heedless of the rain. Riley, in the meantime, was trying to conceive a possible plan to save Kelvin, but any time he thought of something, he second-guessed himself.

"Riley?" Joseph cocked his head a little to the side. "I don't know if you've noticed, but your star is gone. Or, mostly gone."

Riley jerked to a halt. "Huh? Whattaya mean?"

Joseph pointed at Riley's eye.

"Your star. It's almost completely gone."

"What?" Riley's face numbed. "It is?" He started to take out his phone to open the camera. Wait . . . where was his phone? Riley felt inside his pockets, but they were empty.

When did I lose it? Try as he might, Riley couldn't think of where it could possibly be. *I guess it fell out at some point.* Irritated, Riley slapped his pockets and grumbled. His phone was gone and his star was disappearing. What else could go wrong? He tried to recollect what Dorobonn had said about symbols fading. He hadn't been feeling very confident or brave as of late. It then occurred to him—if his star was fading, what did that mean for his magic? All thoughts of his phone aside, Riley focused on a large oak about fifteen feet away and said, "Palstona!"

The fiery ball missed the tree by inches. *Great . . .*

"So, what's the plan?" Joseph asked. He, too, questioned how they were going to accomplish rescuing their friend.

"We're gonna sneak in and find the place where they may have hidden Kelvin. I'll use my magic on the mizzers, if I must."

Joseph didn't say it, but the skepticism in his eyes spoke volumes. How comfortable was Riley with using magic? "We don't even know where they hid him," Joseph said.

"We'll . . ." Riley was also at a loss. "We'll think of something," he said impulsively. He didn't want to admit that he was now questioning himself. It was hard enough to focus on saving their friend when his powers and symbol were diminishing.

The wind picked up.

"You will be betrayed."

"Whoa!" Riley skidded to a halt at the ominous voice. His temple buzzed with pain. *Who said that?*

Only the sound of rustling leaves answered him.

"Riley? Come on!" Joseph called.

Shaking his head, Riley caught up to Joseph. After walking for what felt like an hour or so, the bird alighted on a branch and looked towards a dilapidated cabin behind a grove of trees. Joseph whispered, "I don't believe it. That's it." The moldy wood cracked and flaked in various areas. Three broken windows lined the front. An opening, with broken hinges, led to a dark room. The roof, made of straw, had grayed in many places and crumbled to the ground. What kind of place was this?

"How will we get in without being noticed?" Joseph whispered.

Riley stared hard at the house, trying to assess it. "It's really old-looking, and who knows where the mizzers are? We need to get closer."

They ducked behind some brush and crept around, keeping an eye on the doorway in case someone walked out. They couldn't hear anyone and Riley wondered if this was, in fact, the cabin where Kelvin was being held hostage. The bird had led them here, but what if Riley made a mistake trusting it? After all, it was just a bird. His thoughts were interrupted when Joseph nudged him and pointed at the cabin. A dark-skinned mizzer came out from the doorway. Riley and Joseph snuck behind a large mossy log. The mizzer scanned the forest with his eyes, his face fixed in a glower. He was quite tall and muscular.

"Ardon!" someone called from within the cabin. "Come on, we're having a meeting. Marcus locked Kelvin in The Room."

Kelvin! Riley's stomach flipped.

"Yeah, just makin' sure there weren't any intruders," Ardon spat and went back in.

Riley tapped Joseph's arm and motioned to the side of the cabin. They hurried as soundlessly as they could to the wall and pressed their backs against it. Riley flexed his fingers and formed the word "gaphladeen" in his mind. A small spark crackled in his hand.

"So, do you feel comfortable using your magic on them, if need be?" Joseph asked in a hushed voice.

With a nod, Riley said, "I have to try. It's our only chance." He couldn't fail. Not now.

Riley peeked around the corner of the building but didn't see anyone. He slid alongside the wall and peered in the window. Two mizzers were standing in the middle of the room, talking. The Ardon fellow gazed around lazily. The one standing next to him had pale green eyes, bright red hair reaching past his ears, and was of a similar build.

How in the world would they get past those guys?

"I heard that Kelvin was with two others," Ardon said.

"Yeah. That lil' vampire fellow and the boy who has a star."

Ardon rubbed his chin. "So, the rumors are true, eh? Is he—the one with the star—a human, like they say?"

The other mizzer shrugged indifferently. "Dunno. If he is, that'd be somethin'. A human with a symbol. How does that work?" He smirked. "All three of them are chumps, I gotta tell ya, I've heard that Glazhier—that bloodpire—is after that vampire kid."

"I heard that, too. You know, if we caught that vampire, we could give him to Glazhier. He'd be of no use to us, and maybe we'd even get a reward!"

"What's so special about that boy anyway?"

"I dunno. I heard that he ratted out Glazhier after seeing something the bloodpire was doing."

"Is that so? From what I've heard, that vampire is nothing but a runt. I'm surprised he had the guts to do that."

"According to Kelvin, that . . . what's the vampire kid's name? Eh, no matter. Anyway, Kelvin said he's a bright one. Smart enough to outwit us mizzers."

"Puh! I bet he said that because they're friends. Loyal little . . ."

"Hey, what's that?"

Riley's blood chilled. He'd peered a little further through the window at the same time Ardon looked in his direction. As quick as he could, Riley ducked.

"What's what?"

"I saw something moving."

Sweat beaded the back of Riley's neck. If those mizzers found them out, they'd be goners!

"Who'd come out here, in the middle of nowhere?" the other mizzer scoffed. "Those boys couldn't have followed Solben and them. They don't even know where our hideout is."

Ardon grunted. "I suppose not. Eh, probably just a bird." He and the other mizzer turned away from Riley and Joseph.

"Let's go before Marcus loses his patience," Ardon said and they left through a door which led down a dark stairway.

Riley and Joseph waited a few minutes before going inside. Riley put his hand to the wall but withdrew it after a small splinter stuck into his palm, and he pulled it out. *What a dump.* He put his ear to the door where the two mizzers had gone. Voices sounded below. Who knew how long they'd be down there? Now was their chance! They searched the room, hoping Kelvin hadn't been taken downstairs. The cabin had a wide-open space with furniture everywhere. A fireplace sat in the center of the back wall. Cobwebs draped from the ceiling, and dust was everywhere. How on earth would they find Kelvin in here? Maybe he was downstairs. If so, what chance did they have of freeing him?

"Where *is* he?" Riley sighed, annoyed.

"He has to be somewhere."

"I just hope they didn't take him down to the basement."

Joseph made a grim noise in his throat. "That would be a problem."

Riley sighed. Hot with discomfort and annoyance, he said, "Are we even sure we can rescue Kelvin? What if it's . . . what if we can't?"

Chapter Twenty-Two

Joseph's brows furrowed. "Can't rescue Kelvin? Why would you think that? We've gotten this far. We can't give up!" He gawked. "Your star, Riley. It's—it's gone!"

Riley looked at his reflection in a cracked mirror leaning against the wall and his face drained of color. The star *was* gone.

No. Nooo. Riley touched his eye as a weight pressed on his chest. The burn mark began to ache.

"Riley, here's a door!" Joseph stood before a door which blended in with the rest of the wall. He squinted through the keyhole. "There he is!"

Kelvin—his hands tied behind his back—sat on a chair, head lowered in defeat. Riley jiggled the knob, but the door was locked. "Come—on!"

"Riley?" Kelvin called out quietly. "Joseph? Is that you?"

The hope in Kelvin's voice made Riley more determined than ever to help his friend. "Yes. We're gonna get you out, but we don't know where the key is." Riley yanked at the knob but to no avail.

"Marcus has the key, but you guys don't need to face them. They're too tough and dangerous." Kelvin was silent for a moment. "Hey, Riley!"

"Yeah?" Riley pressed his ear to the keyhole.

"You know magic, right?"

"Umm . . . yeah?"

"You can use it to open the door!"

"What?"

"I said, you can use it to open the door. But be quick! I can hear them coming."

Riley scratched the back of his neck and clutched the knob. "I-I . . . okay."

His scalp suddenly prickled. A tall, dark figure appeared in the forest in his periphery, but when he peered to the side, he didn't see anyone.

Shaking his head, he took a deep breath. "Édian."

Purple flames engulfed the door's hinges, soon melting them. Riley caught the door as it fell forward and placed it against the wall. A sound, which turned Riley's blood cold, came from the stairs. The mizzers were almost to the door!

"Joe, untie Kelvin!" Riley urged. "I'll try to slow them down!"

The back door flew open, and Riley—without thinking twice—shouted, "Gaphladeen!" Lightning shot out of his hand and struck down two of the mizzers. Unfortunately, it fizzled out soon after hitting them and they were standing up again in no time.

"They've released Kelvin! Grab them!" a mizzer with wolfish eyes yelled. Riley had a feeling that was Marcus.

"Riley, hurry!"

The mizzers would catch up to them if nothing was done to stop them. Riley shouted the first word that came to mind.

"Palstona!" The fiery orange sphere missed the mizzers.

They watched as it went into the fireplace. Sparks showered down into the ashes. In a matter of seconds, a fire started and, much to their surprise, swiftly spread through the cabin. Riley —followed by the mizzers—bolted out the door.

Once outside, Riley quickly glanced back over his shoulder. As fire broke through the roof, Riley paused, watching it fan out and engulf the cabin. Palstona had caused more damage than he'd intended. The mizzers—all of whom escaped—had fallen onto the ground, hacking and coughing, covered in ash. Marcus lifted his head and made eye contact with Riley. Resentment burned in his eyes, even hotter than the flames.

"Riley, what're you doing?! C'mon!" Kelvin grabbed him by the shoulders and pulled him back. Startled out of his shock, Riley trailed behind Kelvin and Joseph, away from the flaming cabin.

His heart warned him not to look back, but he risked a glimpse over his shoulder. A column of fire towered over the burnt cabin and formed some sort of dragon creature with its jaws open wide! Its eyes smoldered into Riley's. His body turned hot and then cold. His head hurt, then world went black.

Riley gasped awake and sat up. He rubbed his arms. How long had he been unconscious? Where was the cabin? Was it possible it'd burned down while he was out? If so, where was the fire? The mizzers were nowhere in sight. Legs unsteady, Riley sat on the ground and rubbed the back of his head, wincing. He remembered the dragon from the flames. Where did it come from? Why had he passed out? Sucking in a sharp breath, Riley looked at his palm, on which a raw mark had developed. Weird. Where were Kelvin and Joseph? They hadn't just left him, had they? How would he get back to Zefa? He didn't even know where it was. A chirp greeted him from above. The little green-gold bird looked at him with its head to the side. Though nauseous, Riley rose, stumbling a bit, and followed the bird as it led him to Zefa.

* * *

"The boy's star is gone. If his despair continues, then you will have ample opportunity to rid Leíso of him."

"Indeed. Dorobonn's claim that the third star-bearer will stop me shall come to nothing," Iradocc said to the Vile One as they watched the boy stagger in his attempt to reach Zefa. They were observing him through a mirror of sorts on the wall of the Vile One's chambers. They'd seen the whole incident involving the mizzers. Iradocc's heart swelled with vindictive pleasure. This human child would die because of Dorobonn's selfishness. For all his acting like a saint, Dorobonn was merely a coward. He refused to harm Iradocc in battle. Iradocc wanted a challenge. Hopefully this boy would make a worthy opponent.

Iradocc would NOT let the prophecy come true. He would prove the prophecy wrong, whatever it took. His loathing for the People of the Symbol served as his greatest weapon and made him strong. His parents had always wanted a child with a symbol—particularly a star. They'd hated him for not having one, Iradocc believed. His mother had neglected him half the time. His father, deciding to make Iradocc useful, took it upon himself to train his son in matters of weaponry, and punishing him most harshly when Iradocc became "lazy" or wouldn't listen. Iradocc's brother, on the other hand, had no symbol, and yet, it did not seem to concern his father at all.

"Iradocc."

"Yes, sir?" Iradocc snapped himself back to the present before the Vile One grew suspicious.

"The time has almost arrived." The Vile One's eyes gleamed hungrily.

Later that night, Riley made it back to the castle. He crept to his room, locked his door, and got into bed, full clothed. He tossed and turned, despite his weariness. He couldn't sleep. The moonlight cast unnatural shadows on the walls and ceiling. Tree branches knocked against the window and their shadows took on strange shapes. A dark form stood in the corner. Riley, in a cold sweat, lurched back, banging his head against the headboard. The figure didn't move. If only he had a flashlight or a light switch! The oil lamp sat beside his bed. He turned the key and held it up.

The "figure" was a coat rack. Riley slumped against the bed frame with a slow sigh. He couldn't take it anymore! His mind wouldn't let him sleep. Shuffling out of bed, he went to the door and walked out of the room. Something didn't feel right.

Chapter Twenty-Three

"And just what do you think you're doing?"

The voice nearly scared Riley half to death! He turned around, finding Matthew standing only inches away from him with a lantern in his hand. How long had he been there?

"I hope you are not going outside. It's too dangerous after dark," Matthew said.

Recovering his speech, Riley replied, "Yeah, well . . . I was . . ."

"By the way, Edilie told me you disobeyed my orders and left Zefa. Pray tell me why?"

Riley searched for a plausible answer. He wouldn't be intimidated by Matthew any longer, and yet he wanted to be careful. Who knew what the steward had up his sleeve?

"I was taking a little walk. Iradocc is coming and I need to be prepared."

"How do you know Iradocc will attack Zefa?"

Riley hadn't expected *that* question. "What do you mean?"

"Have you been communicating with him?" Now Matthew's tone took on a sharper edge.

"In a manner of speaking. He's been threatening me and threatened to destroy Zefa. I can't ignore that."

"And what makes you think *you* can stop him?"

"Because only a person with a symbol can defeat him."

"How do you know a *Human Worlder* can beat him? A Human Worlder *child*, no less?" Where was Matthew going with these questions?

"Because that's what the prophecy says and what Dorobonn told me."

"How do you know Dorobonn is trustworthy and that the prophecy is even true?"

This interrogation was getting on Riley's nerves, and why did both Edilie and Matthew have a problem with Dorobonn? "He's not a bad guy, if that's what you're asking," Riley said defensively. "He's my mentor and he said that Iradocc destroyed the People of the Symbol—I know *that's* true. Iradocc wants to get rid of me. Now, if you'll excuse me, I need to return to bed," Riley said, unable to resist adding mockery to his tone. He brushed past Matthew and, once inside his room, locked the door. First thing tomorrow morning, he would visit Dorobonn.

Riley took his breakfast into his room and reflected on Matthew's behavior. He suspected that Matthew had ties with Dark Magic, he just didn't know exactly what those ties were. He had no solid proof. Finishing his breakfast, Riley went outside. On the way to Dorobonn's, the forest became eerily quiet. The creaking of a tree made him jump. He shivered as a gust of wind blew through his hair. *The cabin's not far.*

Dorobonn's house was just on the edge of the forest. Try as he might to keep himself calm, Riley became more agitated with each step.

He heard something behind him. Beads of sweat tickled Riley's brow. Slowly, he turned his head.

A bolt of black lightning sped right at him and knocked him directly into a tree. Riley landed with an "oomph!" on the ground. A man with stringy black hair framing a long pasty-skinned face, and orange eyes, glared at him. Filthy, tattered clothing covered his skeletal body. *What the . . . ?*

The man snarled, showing razor-sharp teeth. Had *he* shot the lightning at Riley? Riley's chest stung, bad. He looked at his burn mark. The mark turned the color of an ugly bruise.

The man hissed, and threw a blue spear of flame straight at Riley.

Riley darted to the side. "Who are you?" he screamed, backing away.

"Someone who was sent to destroy you," the creature ground out, licking his teeth, and then moved his hand in a circle in the air. A thin sword appeared. Intricate designs of swirls and strange symbols were carved into the handle.

Riley yelled, "Gaphladeen!" but the lightning didn't come.

"Palstona!" Nothing.

The demolic grinned. His sword turned dark purple, with flames emanating from the tip.

How in the world am I supposed to fight him? Riley glanced everywhere for a weapon or a way out.

The demolic appeared beside him and swung the blade for his throat.

Riley ducked in the nick of time.

I can't fight him! I can't fight him!

Flustered, Riley yelled, "Édian!"

It proved useless! Why wouldn't his powers work?

The demolic kicked him in the stomach, making him fall to the ground and pointed his sword at Riley's heart.

Gasping, Riley scrambled back.

"How strong are you?" the demolic hissed, and stabbed the sword forward, but Riley rolled out of the way and tried to stand, but not before the demolic stomped his boot on Riley's chest, pinning him to the ground. The demolic crouched, placing his knees on Riley's arms. He held the edge of the blade against Riley's throat and smiled grotesquely.

"Unlucky boy. I haven't had this much fun in years! No need to struggle, *human*. You can't get out of this."

"Óra!" another voice shouted.

A beam of crystalline light smote the demolic. He rolled off of Riley and then laid still, disappearing in a dark fog.

Riley whipped around and, to his relief, saw Dorobonn, who walked up to him and held out his hand. Riley accepted it and got up. "Thanks," he said with a weak smile.

Dorobonn observed Riley with penetrating eyes. "Why didn't you use your magic?"

Riley lowered his head. "I tried, but nothing happened!"

There was silence for a moment until Dorobonn said quietly, "Your star. It has faded. Your magic is fading. You are losing courage."

Riley didn't argue. Lifting his eyes to the sky, he grumbled, "Why is it so hard for me to be brave? When I think I've got it all figured out, I mess up. What's wrong with me?"

"There's nothing wrong with you, Riley. We all make mistakes. When that happens, we must face our fears and push through the obstacles. It's hard, I know, but you can't let those problems stop you from fighting for what you know is right. We must keep improving ourselves."

"But when I try, I mess things up."

"Explain."

"Kelvin was kidnapped by the mizzers recently and Joseph and I went to save him. We did . . . but the mizzers tried to catch us and I used my magic on them. My magic set their hideout on fire. No one died! But in the flames, I saw the form of a terrible dragon. It looked at me, and then I passed out. When I woke up, I didn't know where Kelvin and Joseph were."

The entire time Riley told his story, Dorobonn watched him—his expression was hard to read. "You were saving your friend?"

"Yeah. But I don't know where that dragon came from."

"Dragons are dangerous. What you saw may have been a result of, not your magic, but something darker. Your intentions were good. You were rescuing a friend. The dragon was very likely a mix of the distress and desperation you felt at the time. It has happened before, people seeing forms of dragons, or some other terrible creature, when they feel lost or in great despair."

Riley let that sink in. Was he only one who had seen the dragon? The thought frightened him more than he'd like to admit. "How did you find your way back to the village?" Dorobonn asked.

"A bird. It showed me the way just as it showed Joseph and me the way when we began searching for Kelvin."

Dorobonn tapped his chin with his forefinger. "Fascinating." He then asked the question Riley dreaded to answer. "What of your friend Caroline? Is she back safely in the Human World?"

Swallowing hard, Riley fidgeted with his shirt collar. "Caroline? She . . . er." How could he tell Dorobonn that she'd been captured?

"Is everything alright, son? You look sick."

"Ah . . . she . . . and Lunaira were . . . uh, kidnapped."

"Kidnapped?" Though quietly spoken, the word sounded like an exclamation to Riley's ears. He flinched.

"By whom?"

"Iradocc," Riley muttered.

"Iradocc took Caroline and the princess?" The green in Dorobonn's eyes darkened.

He nodded slowly, wanting the ground to swallow him up. The shame he felt was almost unbearable and made him wish that he'd never come to Leíso in the first place. "Yes," he murmured.

"Did you not warn her like I told you to?"

Mouth dry, Riley subtly shook his head. "I mean . . . I did . . . but . . . I . . ."

His mentor's gaze drilled into him. Riley's shoulders sank, as did his heart.

"What happened, Riley?" The disappointment in Dorobonn's tone hit Riley square in the stomach.

Why? Why?! Why?! *Why didn't I warn Caroline? What's the matter with me? I'm so stupid!* "I . . . I practiced my magic before I told her anything. I did warn her afterwards," he said hastily. "She didn't listen . . ."

He dared a peek at Dorobonn. His mentor's expression said it all. If Riley had talked to Caroline as soon as possible, all of this could have been avoided. "Oh, Riley."

Riley couldn't help asking, "What . . . what was the danger I had to keep Caroline from? Iradocc said that he'd trapped Caroline and Lunaira in Ellúciena. Where is that place? Why would he do that?"

"Ellúciena? It is a place of nightmares. It muddles one's mind. Why did you not warn her when I told you to?"

Riley rubbed his forehead, gritting his teeth. "I . . ." Filled with aggravation, he burst out, "You always act so mysterious! You didn't tell me why I needed to warn her! If I know Caroline, she probably wouldn't have listened, anyway. You don't know her like I do." His heart skipped a beat at Dorobonn's frown, and he knew he'd crossed a line. He also recalled his and Caroline's argument before the kidnapping. It had been similar, except, Caroline had accused Riley of being secretive and suggested they shouldn't be friends. Not only that, but she'd said he really didn't know her as well as he thought he did.

"There is no time to waste, child," Dorobonn said firmly. "You must be prepared for your battle."

Riley wished now, more than ever, that he'd stayed in the Human World. He felt like the biggest coward of all time. "Dorobonn? The book . . . it's no longer there. At the castle, I mean."

Dorobonn stared at him in silence. "It's not?"

"No. I asked the steward, Matthew, if he knew where it was. He wouldn't tell me."

"The book is no longer important," Dorobonn said after a moment or two.

"It . . . why?"

"You've learned what you needed from it. Now is the time to move ahead. Just what else did Matthew have to say to you?"

"Nothing else, but I did overhear him mention the name of their guest to Lunaira. Sir Leod."

"Sir Leod? The Golden Knight. He's a terrible man, if you can even call him that. He murdered Jerith, Edilie's grandfather."

"Edilie? You mean, the guard at the Zefan castle?"

"Aye. Sir Leod goes by Remadof now. Sir Leod was his former name. Jerith was in the service of Lunaira's grandfather and his abilities as a mighty warrior happened to catch Sir Leod's eye. Sir Leod had begun working for the Vile One by that time. I was there when Sir Leod battled Jerith—who was a friend of mine. Jerith had refused to serve the Vile One. Sir

Leod fatally wounded my friend in battle. I tried to save him but to no avail. His son, Edilie's father, was hardhearted and did not believe me when I told him what had happened. He insisted that I was somehow to blame for his father's death."

"Wasn't he angry at all with Sir—Remadof?" Riley exclaimed indignantly.

"I do not know. Edilie's father was narrow-minded and since I was there at the time of the battle, he had the notion that I should have saved his father, as I was a magician. Clearly, he was not aware of the evil that Remadof was capable of." Dorobonn sighed. "Now that Remadof is here, our situation with Dark Magic has become worse. *He* may have somehow had a hand in Caroline and Lunaira's capture."

"What . . ." Riley bit his lip. "What'll Iradocc do to Caroline and Lunaira if I don't rescue them in time? I don't know how long I have."

"He may be planning to keep them imprisoned forever, but I am not certain. Go back to the castle. I fear Iradocc will strike soon. You cannot waste any time!"

"What about you? Won't you help me?"

The kindness in Dorobonn's eyes calmed Riley. "I will be there when you need me."

Chapter Twenty-Four

As he headed for the castle, Riley looked at the sky. The clouds were a strange deep blue and greenish color. The air sizzled with electricity. Castle guards ordered the villagers to stay inside their homes until the storm passed, murmuring about the ominous clouds looking unlike anything they had ever seen.

When would Iradocc arrive? Not knowing that made Riley's stomach feel like lead.

"I said no riffraff in the castle. You have no business here."

Riley turned his head, seeing Kelvin and Joseph in an argument with Edilie.

"We're here to see Riley. We know he wouldn't mind us visiting," Kelvin retorted, crossing his arms defiantly.

"He has no say in who can or cannot enter the castle," Edilie snapped. "If you do not leave this instant, I will set my guards on you and have them *escort* you out of the village."

"I don't think so," Riley said. He noticed Edilie tightening his grip on his spear. "You're paranoid, Edilie. You don't trust me, I get it. They're my friends and I need their help."

Edilie sneered. "Matthew will hear of your rebellious behavior. After that, it'll be the cells for you."

"Do what you want. Matthew has no authority over me. And if you put me in a cell, you will lose your only chance at keeping Iradocc from destroying everyone and everything."

Edilie lowered his spear, but then grabbed Riley by the shirtfront. "*You're* no warrior. Iradocc is attacking Zefa because of *you*." He squinted. "What is happening to your star?"

"It's . . . a long story," Riley sighed, not bothering to hide his frustration with the guard.

Edilie snorted. "This world doesn't need any more symbols anyway. Nor does it need any more Human Worlders." He marched back to his troop.

Riley smoothed out his shirt and then faced his friends. "Follow me." He led them to his room inside the castle. Matthew was nowhere in sight. Locking his door, Riley sat on his bed. Kelvin leaned against the wall while Joseph rested in a chair.

"Thanks for the save, mate," Kelvin said. "We've been looking for you! We asked that disagreeable guard if he knew where you were, but he said that, since we're your friends, we should leave, if we knew what was good for us."

Are you kidding me? "He's been that way towards me ever since Caroline and I came to Zefa."

Kelvin fidgeted with his hat. "In his words, that mentor of yours—that Dorobonn fellow—is a magician with unspeakable Dark Magic. *We* don't believe that. I don't know about the villagers. We've been hearing whispers about how you are the reason for that Cloud."

Riley fell back on his bed, groaning aloud. Was there any way to prove his innocence?

A fire suddenly kindled in Riley's heart. A fire he had not felt before. "I can't give up. If I do, Iradocc will kill me and the

Vile One will take over, not only Leíso, but the Human World as well, forever."

Chapter Twenty-Five

"The Vile One?" Kelvin asked, cocking his head. "You mean the one who lives in Haedian?"

"Yeah. Him. I've met him before, in the Human World. He tried to convince me to work for him, but I wouldn't."

"Are you gonna battle him, too?"

"No. Only Iradocc."

"Is there anything we can do to help?" Joseph asked.

Riley shook his head. "No. This is up to me. I don't want you guys to get hurt, or worse, killed. Caroline and Lunaira have already been kidnapped by Iradocc because of me, so I'm not going to risk causing anything to happen to you two, as well."

"Are you ready to battle him?" Kelvin questioned, somewhat hesitantly.

Riley swallowed hard before answering, "I . . . I hope so. I wish I had more time to train, but that's not gonna happen."

"Just when *is* this battle between you and Iradocc going to occur?"

Riley slowly turned and stared out the window as the dark storm clouds began to gradually cover the sun and cast their surroundings in shadow. "Any time now."

Chapter Twenty-Six

A feeling of foreboding came over Riley. He opened the window and saw streaks of lightning reaching across the sky, like claws. Loud cracks of thunder split the air and the wind began to pick up.

"Go find Dorobonn! Tell him that Iradocc's here," Riley urged. He could feel the presence of Dark Magic in the room. Heavy and almost stifling.

Kelvin and Joseph left without another word.

"At last," a snide voice said, echoing throughout the room. "Ever since you came to Leíso, I have been anticipating my opportunity to destroy you."

Riley took a deep breath as he turned to see Iradocc standing behind him. The demolic's eyes flickered in the shadows like fire and cold as ice. The curved blade Riley had seen in his nightmare glinted in the dim light.

"You are the last person with a symbol," Iradocc said. "*I* will see to it that you are the *very* last."

Riley's heart began to hammer. "I won't let you win, Iradocc."

"*Won't*? You are overconfident, boy," Iradocc snorted. "I must say, I was not expecting the third star–bearer to be a *Human Worlder*. You are a curious creature. Anyone with any intelligence, much less a Human Worlder, would not dare face a demolic in battle, but *you*, with your foolish attempt at courage, seem willing."

"You froze my family, kidnapped Caroline and the princess, wiped out the People of the Symbol, and you'll do the same to Althia!"

"Do you think I care one way or the other about your family or friends, or Althia? *You* are an obstacle which needs to be disposed of! I will not let the prophecy come true!" Iradocc roared and stabbed the blade forward. Riley sidestepped the weapon and ran out of the room.

"Run all you want, boy! I *will* catch you eventually."

I need to fight him in a place where he can't hurt anyone!

"Orsyth!"

Riley glanced over his shoulder to see a column of fire speeding at him. Falling to the floor, Riley covered his head as the flames smashed into the door. Dripping with sweat, he scrambled to his feet and made for the forest.

"What's happening?!" Edilie demanded, spotting Riley, who ran past him.

"I can't explain right now, Edilie! Tell everyone to stay inside!" Riley didn't stop until he was far out of sight of the village. He didn't dare look back to see if Iradocc was following him. After what felt like hours, Riley paused with his hands on his knees, gasping. He needed a plan. A strategy of sorts. The entire sky was dark with storm clouds, except for the occasional flash of lightning.

"Running away, are we?"

Riley's body prickled. He pressed his back to a tree

and looked around. Where was Iradocc? "Are you afraid, child?"

"N-no."

"No? Indeed. You *sound* afraid."

"I-I'm not!" Riley cringed, wishing he didn't sound so nervous. "I . . . there's no reason f-for me to be afraid of you."

"Is there not?" Iradocc scoffed.

How could he find Iradocc when he was invisible? *Focus. I have to focus!* "Gaphladeen!" The crimson lightning struck Iradocc, who turned visible, in the shoulder.

Cradling his shoulder, Iradocc grinned coldly. "Excellent. A challenge is just what I am looking for." He slashed his sword, covered in blue fire, at Riley. Riley jumped out of the way as the tree behind him crashed to the ground. He got to his feet, yelling "gaphladeen!" again, distracting Iradocc, and then ran.

How could he fight a madman? "Come on, boy! I came here for a fight and you're running like a coward! You gave the impression that you were willing to do this."

Would my magic even work against him? He's more powerful than me. What can I do?!

"Enough of this! Írloch!" Screeching to a halt, Riley watched as flames encircled the forest with him and Iradocc in the middle. His heart raced. "If you will not fight, then I will kill you here and now!" Iradocc said.

I can't let him win. I can't! "Palstona!" Iradocc *grabbed* the ball and crushed it! "Édian!" Not even that power seemed to have any effect. Riley backed away until he could feel the heat from the wall of flames.

Iradocc fingered his blade. "I suppose you are not as worthy of an opponent as I had hoped."

Seeing a large tree out of his peripheral, Riley dashed for it, hoping that, perhaps if he climbed high enough, he could find a way over the wall of fire. He leapt for the closest branch and clambered on to it.

"What are you doing, boy? Trying to escape? Ha! You are more foolish than I thought!" Iradocc slashed at each branch Riley mounted. Once or twice Riley narrowly missed grabbing a branch and almost fell to the ground. He had not realized just how high he had climbed until he was almost directly above Iradocc's head. Riley moved over to the branch next to him, which barely held his weight. He looked, but there were no other branches close by.

The tree shook violently. Riley held on tight and looked down, seeing Iradocc bury the curved sword into the wood. That was enough to start a crack, which tore through the trunk. He was cutting down the entire tree! Riley gasped and looked over his shoulder at the fire. Where else could he go? A loud cracking sound made his heart stop.

The tree fell in the direction of the fire! Riley hurried to the other side of the tree away from the flames and, holding on, braced himself for the searing heat. The wind was knocked out of him as the tree hit the ground and he rolled off. Riley scrambled back as Iradocc stepped through the fire, his eyes snapping impatiently. "Fight like a man!" Grabbing a root from a fallen tree next to him, Iradocc stretched it out like clay! He tossed the root and then another in Riley's direction and they came for him, slithering towards him on the ground. One started to wrap around his leg but he pulled away and ran. Not just tree roots, but now thorns and vines reached for him. It wasn't long before they surrounded him and the thorns pierced his arms as they circled his body. The tree roots wrapped around him, holding him tight. Riley kicked and jerked, but in vain. Iradocc approached and Riley was lifted face–to–face with him. He held the curved blade to Riley's throat.

"If you had cooperated, your death would have been quick

and painless. Well, perhaps not 'painless.'" Iradocc took Riley's chin in his hand, satisfied. "Your symbol is fading, and soon, you will, too."

The tree roots lowered allowing Iradocc to press the sword against Riley's shirt. Riley sucked in a sharp breath as the fabric came apart, revealing his burn mark. Iradocc placed the tip of the blade on the burn mark. As he did so, the roots tightened around Riley, crushing his lungs, making it difficult to breathe.

Can't . . . can't . . . no! Riley gritted his teeth.

"Elomé made a mistake with you. You are worthless."

Something inside Riley snapped at those words. He recalled what Dorobonn had said—Elomé never made mistakes. Clenching his fists, Riley summoned what little strength he had and looked Iradocc in the eye. He could feel his symbol returning.

"You're wrong. Elomé is with me!"

Iradocc hesitated a second before sneering and replied, "You have no courage left. Your magic is useless."

"Because I was afraid. But not anymore! Elomé Doesn't. Make. Mistakes!" Riley grabbed the tree roots and braced himself. Iradocc backed away, doubtful.

"*Gaphladeen*!" The roots vibrated, crackled, and then exploded. Riley landed on all fours, gasping. He staggered to his feet and looked at Iradocc. "No matter what, I'll fight for this world and the Human World. Elomé is by my side. Always."

Riley thought he detected a note of astonishment in Iradocc's eyes, but it vanished quickly. "Is that so? And how can you be so sure?" Iradocc said. "You're only a human child in a world full of secrets beyond your comprehension—Dark Magic being one of them. You know not in what you meddle."

"And you know very little about me," Riley replied. "As I said—I'm not afraid of you!"

"Let us test that, shall we?" Iradocc growled. Both of his swords crackled with fire and lightning. In spite of Iradocc's words, Riley could tell the demolic was beginning to weaken.

"Palstona! Gaphladeen!" He would keep at it until Iradocc gave out. Iradocc, it seemed, was struggling to keep up with Riley's repeated attacks. Vexed with how little progress he was making, Iradocc threw his curved sword at Riley. It almost slashed Riley in the ribs, but he jumped to the side, avoiding it as it flew past him. Trembling with rage, Iradocc stabbed his other sword at Riley, who cried, "Ilíeanda!" a word he had not actually yet used. Iradocc's sword crumbled to dust and he was left only with the handle.

Iradocc stared at it in shock. "How—?! This is not possible!"

Upon hearing Iradocc's exclamation, Riley lowered his arm and he, too, looked at the handle in astonishment. Iradocc turned a furious glare on Riley. "What did you do?"

Riley held up his hands. "I . . . I don't think I did anything."

"Liar!" Iradocc searched for his curved sword, which was not far from Riley. As quickly as possible, Riley snatched it before Iradocc could find it. The demolic *was* getting slower. Riley pointed it at Iradocc, thinking perhaps now he had the upper-hand.

"You think you can wield a sword forged in Haedian?" Iradocc said. "I am its Master; it will only listen to me."

"Listen"? What does he mean? Suddenly, the burn mark began to radiate pain so severe that Riley clinched his fist to it and gritted his teeth to keep from crying out. He sank to his knees.

"Have you forgotten, foolish child, that your burn mark is the same image as that blade in your hand?" Iradocc scorned. "You can't fight me with a weapon that only responds to . . . Me."

Riley didn't want to let go of the sword, for then Iradocc would use it against him, but what choice did he have? Reluctantly, he dropped it and, after a moment, the pain from his burn mark abated.

"Smart boy," Iradocc said, picking up the blade. He then kicked Riley in the ribs and pinned him to the ground by his shoulder. "It is time I put an end to this battle."

"I forgive you, Iradocc!" The words were not Riley's. They both turned and saw Dorobonn standing, but a few feet away.

"Dorobonn! What are *you* doing here? This battle is between the boy and me." Doubt showed in Iradocc's gaze. "You . . . what did you just say?"

"I forgive you, Iradocc. Cease your need for vengeance. It is a poison which will only destroy you."

Iradocc straightened, but kept his sword aimed at Riley's heart. "I do not want your forgiveness. I wish to wipe you and this boy from existence."

"Regardless," Dorobonn said calmly, "I bear no ill will against you."

Iradocc's brows furrowed. "You have always been a soft-hearted fool, Dorobonn."

"Say what you will. I am now rid of the burn mark you gave me all those years ago." Dorobonn pulled down his collar and there, the burn mark had healed! Iradocc looked on in amazement. For a moment Riley thought he detected a hint of regret in Iradocc's expression. It vanished in an instant.

He turned his attention to Riley. "I care not. This boy is a threat to me and I won't let him live any longer!"

"Lúra!" A shield of sorts covered Riley, shimmering with light when the sword struck it.

Iradocc faced Dorobonn. "You failed to save the People of the Symbol. And I am about to make your failure complete!"

He ran at Dorobonn and slammed into him, knocking him to the ground. Iradocc lifted his sword over Dorobonn's heart.

Riley yelled, "I forgive you!"

Iradocc faltered and then turned to Riley. Riley felt curious sensation at the site of his burn mark was—like a scar healing. He looked down. It was gone!

All of a sudden, the curved blade in Iradocc's hand began to quiver. All three of them stared as the sword trembled violently and then suddenly burst into pieces. Riley gawked. Iradocc looked hard at his hand where the sword had been.

"How is this . . . how could this . . . why . . .?"

"You know why the sword broke, Iradocc. Its power has faded. Stop following this path of darkness. It will eventually bring about your own ruin."

Iradocc fisted his hands, struggling with himself. "No. I . . . I must go back to Haedian. I will replenish my powers—strengthen them." He looked at Riley. "I will not cease my quest for vengeance until you are gone!" Turning on Dorobonn, he said, "You cannot understand my pain. You never will! As children, our parents made it clear that I would never live up to their expectations. They said I was nothing but a disappointment. I will come for you once I have grown stronger again!" Iradocc then disappeared in a dark mist.

* * *

THEIR parents? Are Iradocc and Dorobonn . . . brothers?! Riley paled at this revelation. Dorobonn bowed his head, weary. Riley looked up at the sky and noticed the cloud was gone. But why didn't he feel like celebrating?

Chapter Twenty-Seven

"Riley!" Startled out of his thoughts Riley whirled around and spotted Kelvin running through the woods towards them, a look of panic on his face.

"Kelvin! What's up?"

"It's Joe. I can't find him! We went to Dorobonn's house after we left the castle, but when we . . . well, when *I* got there, he wasn't with me. I've been searching for him. I think . . ."

Riley knew what Kelvin was afraid of. Glazhier capturing Joseph. If so, Joseph didn't stand a chance. Riley grumbled. Why did this have to happen? First Iradocc and now Glazhier!

"What is wrong?" Dorobonn asked.

"My friend Joseph and I were coming to your cabin, sir, when Riley and Iradocc were battling. But when I got to the house, Joseph wasn't with me. I think Glazhier has him!"

Dorobonn's eyes flashed. "We must hurry and find him! We have no time to lose."

They scoured the forest. Riley cried out "Joseph!" several times, but with no response. After what felt like hours, Riley came upon a small cavern deep in the woods leading underground. He went inside. Roots hung from the ceiling and water trickled down the walls.

"Hold still, you little rat!"

Riley clambered faster down the tunnel, attempting to keep from slipping as he made his way through the darkness. If he wasn't mistaken, that was Glazhier's voice, and no doubt the "little rat" he spoke to, was Joseph! He came to a small opening in the wall of the cave which was just large enough for him to step through. Upon entering what looked like some kind of underground chamber, Riley saw that Glazhier had Joseph cornered with his back to the wall. Glazhier's gaunt hand hovered over Joseph's forehead. Joseph screamed in pain.

"*Gaphladeen*!" Riley shouted the word impulsively, without thinking. The lightning struck Glazhier, head-on! He crashed into the wall and fell to the floor. Riley slid into the room and ran to Joseph, who was on the ground, holding his head.

"Joe? Joe, it's me, Riley!"

Joseph sat up, gasping. "Riley? Agh!" He squeezed his eyes shut and held his middle. Riley glanced at the bloodpire, still lying on the ground. What had Glazhier done to Joseph?

"Let's get outta here." Putting an arm around Joseph's shoulders, Riley helped him up. Joseph stumbled as he rose but Riley kept a tight grip on his friend and began leading him out of the chamber towards the tunnel.

"You think you can just take my victim and leave?"

Riley peered over his shoulder. Glazhier slowly stood up, glowering at them, his face full of wrath.

The room began to shudder, like in an earthquake. Cracks formed in the ground and made their way up the walls. Riley turned and faced Glazhier, whose arms were spread wide as he cast his spell. Riley's hands crackled with red electricity and gleaming fire.

"There will be no escape for you *or* your puny little friend! You're no match for me!" the bloodpire jeered.

"Palstona!" Riley yelled. Glazhier sidestepped the ball of fire before it could hit him. "Gaphladeen!" The lightning found its mark. "You'll have to go through *me* first!"

"If that is your wish." The bloodpire's eyes glinted and the ground began to split underneath Riley.

"Stop this at once, Glazhier!" The voice belonged to Dorobonn. He and Kelvin appeared in the doorway. Dorobonn caused the earthquake to come to a halt, overcoming Glazhier's powers. Kelvin knelt next to Joseph. Dorobonn walked past Riley, and looked hard at Glazhier. "Begone, Glazhier! Your magic is weakening."

The bloodpire scowled at Dorobonn and then at Riley, Kelvin, and Joseph. "I see I cannot win this fight at this moment, but mark my words—I will return for that vampire runt!" Glazhier declared, piercing Joseph with his sinister gaze. Immediately transforming into a bat, he flew out the tunnel. All was quiet when he left. Dorobonn looked at Joseph.

"Are you alright, son?" he asked gently. Joseph gave him a brisk nod. "Yes, sir."

The pain he'd felt earlier had disappeared and he was able to walk himself out of the cavern. Riley explained to Dorobonn what Glazhier had done. Dorobonn listened with a grave expression. "There is more to Glazhier's motives than you might think," he said. "Not only does Glazhier wish to destroy your friend, but he also wishes to steal Joseph's ability from him."

"Steal it? Why? Can he do that?"

"His Dark Magic is very ancient in origin. It gives him the ability to extract magical powers from others. It is a form of torture which was used many years ago on Light Magicians.

Has Joseph told you the story behind Glazhier's hatred for him?"

"Yes, sir."

"And has Joseph told you that his ability does not work on Glazhier?"

Riley wavered. "He . . . he didn't." The more he thought about it, the more Riley realized that's why Glazhier was able to attack Joseph. Otherwise, his friend would've frozen Glazhier on the spot and escaped on his own. "But *why* would he want to steal Joseph's ability?"

"It is a very rare and desirable magic, and Glazhier wishes it for himself. Clearly, he will go to whatever lengths he feels necessary to attain it. You must be sure to keep Joseph safe." When they arrived at Zefa, Dorobonn smiled at Riley. "You have shown great courage today, my son."

Riley's face flushed. "Thanks. I tried to be brave against Iradocc. Battling him . . ."

"Forgiving him is what I'm referring to. *That* took bravery. Not many would forgive their enemies. You have more courage than you think."

"I used gaphladeen on Glazhier twice and it hit him. I had a harder time with it as I fought Iradocc."

"That is why. You were willing to forgive Iradocc and it strengthened your will and your powers. You were better prepared to save your friend. Relying solely on your magic isn't always the best solution. There are other ways to win a fight, and not merely by magic."

Riley smiled, his face growing warm. Lifting his eyes to the castle, a grim feeling settled in his gut and his smile faded. "Iradocc said he'd free Caroline, Lunaira, and my family. Why do I get the feeling that he didn't keep his word?"

Dorobonn's expression grew sad. "If I know Iradocc, he will not stay true to his word."

Disturbing as Dorobonn's response was, Riley had known in his heart that the fight was far from over. And yet, Iradocc's words to Dorobonn were perplexing. Uncomfortable about bringing it up, Riley said, "You and Iradocc are *brothers* . . .??"

"Aye."

"He . . . he almost killed you, even though you had just forgiven him."

Dorobonn was silent for a moment before answering. "Yes, he did *intend* to kill me, but he could not bring himself to. I saw it in his eyes."

"Do you think he would've if I hadn't forgiven him at that moment?"

"The Dark Magic has a strong hold on Iradocc . . . it is impossible to say."

Chapter Twenty-Eight

Riley ran and swung open the doors to the castle, hoping against hope that Caroline and Lunaira were safely back after all. Dorobonn had said that he needed to return to his cabin. He'd not explained why, but it seemed urgent and he had assured Riley that he would not be long. With Kelvin and Joseph's help, Riley searched the castle up and down, ignoring the protests of the staff. Word must have reached Edilie of their activity, for the guard confronted Riley as Riley hastened from room to room.

"What is the meaning of this?!" he demanded, blocking Riley's path.

"I'm trying to find Caroline and the princess! Iradocc said he would free them."

Edilie looked puzzled. "They're not here. Where is Iradocc?"

Riley's heart sank low. "I . . . I fought him. And won the battle. He won't be bothering Zefa anymore."

"*You* beat Iradocc?" Edilie said in a quiet voice. "How . . ."

Footsteps drew near.

"No luck finding Caroline or the princess," Joseph said. Riley's shoulders drooped. He should've known better than to have held out any belief that Iradocc would have freed them.

"Wait for me outside. Dorobonn said he'd be back soon." When Riley and Edilie were alone in the hall, Riley asked him, "Do you know where Matthew is?"

"No. He disappeared shortly before you fought Iradocc."

"Matthew said a guest was coming. Sir Leod."

Edilie's face lost color. "Yes. I saw him."

"You . . . *saw* him?"

Edilie acted as though he wished to forget what he had seen. "Aye. He and Matthew were in the study. I overheard them talking. After they finished, I made myself scarce. When Sir Leod spoke, his voice sounded like that of a snake. Cunning and poisonous."

So Matthew *was* in league with *them*. "What were they talking about?"

Edilie peered at the ground, uncertain.

"Please, Edilie," Riley said. "I have to know."

"They discussed you, that magician fellow, Dorobonn, and Dark Magic."

"Do you know what, exactly, was said?"

"Sir Leod told Matthew that if *you* overcame Iradocc in battle (which was quite unlikely), then the Vile One would not hesitate to do whatever was necessary to stop you from freeing the other kingdoms of Dark Magic. The same would apply to Dorobonn as well. Sir Leod sounded eager to confront Dorobonn regarding something (I know not what) that Dorobonn had done to him in the past. Matthew said that since *you* were a Human Worlder, it shouldn't be too difficult to get rid of you. And no, they spoke nothing of her majesty or the young lady."

The very idea of the Vile One doing "whatever was necessary" to conquer Leíso made Riley's skin crawl and to feel more anxious than ever to rescue his family and friends.

"If you ask me, this mission will prove fruitless," Edilie said. "A person with a symbol who is despised by others is bound to fail. Much less a Human Worlder."

"What makes you say that?"

"People with symbols are traitorous," said Edilie, his gaze hardening. "Human Worlders are insufferable."

This seemed to be a typical Zefan mindset. "Edilie, why don't you trust people with symbols or Human Worlders?"

The guard scowled.

"My father taught me that the People of the Symbol were dangerous. Human Worlders notwithstanding."

"Why?"

"The idea of symbols has always been an anomaly in the Kingdom of Althia. There are stories about people with symbols. Stories which I dare not repeat that my father told me as a child. All I *can* say is that they were depicted as cunning and deceitful. Willing to hurt others for their own gain. As for Human Worlders; my father has had dealings with Human Worlders. Unsavory men. Cheaters and liars."

Riley wondered where those stories about people with symbols originated. Did Dorobonn know anything about them? "No one's told me yet how many humans you've had come to Leíso."

Ironically, Edilie seemed at a loss for an answer. "One of the kings of Zefa was a human, years ago. Before him, Leíso history mentions humans every now and again."

"And do you really see me as no different than those others?"

Edilie absently twisted his spear in his hand. "I . . . if you must know, I do. After that battle with Iradocc, I can see you are no mere coward or liar."

Riley gave him a small smile. His mind then turned to Iradocc. "Dorobonn warned me that Iradocc wouldn't keep his word concerning freeing Caroline and Princess Lunaira. I will let him know what you told me about Sir Leod and Matthew's conversation."

Edilie stiffened and Riley said, "I know you don't trust Dorobonn, but you have to give him a chance. You *can* trust him."

The guard didn't seem convinced but he didn't argue. "If you say so. I, too, will lend a hand in whatever way I can."

Riley had not expected that. "Thanks. Dorobonn said he'll be back soon. I'm gonna go outside and wait for him."

The villagers, as Riley met up with his friends outside the castle, flocked to him and asked about Iradocc and the Dark Magic.

"Is the Dark Magic gone?"

"Where is Iradocc?"

"Did *you* fight him?"

Riley looked at each and every face surrounding him and said, "Yes. The Dark Magic is gone. I won the battle with Iradocc." Riley observed the sky, as did everyone else. "The Cloud has disappeared. You're all free." Everyone glanced at each other in amazed silence. An excited murmur rippled through the crowd which soon erupted into cheering.

A celebration soon began, but Riley, wanting to get away from the crowd, slipped into the forest with Kelvin and Joseph trailing behind. He was happy for the people but his heart was heavy. Why was Dorobonn taking so long?

"Whatcha thinking about, mate?" Kelvin asked as he sat on a stump.

"Where's Dorobonn? He said he'd be back soon a while ago."

* * *

It was midnight. The party had dispersed earlier than evening, but Dorobonn still hadn't shown up. Moon shadows clustered around them and a faint breeze touched Riley's face. Joseph yawned. Kelvin had already fallen asleep.

"'ello, young'uns!"

Riley jumped at the voice. Kelvin nearly fell off of the stump he'd been sitting on.

"Alan!" Riley exclaimed, seeing the ghost approaching them from the direction of the Endless Field. He glowed grey-blue and his eyes twinkled amiably.

"It's been a while, my lad," Alan said. "'ow've you been, eh? I 'ear you battled Iradocc and won. Quite an accomplishment, lad. Quite an accomplishment!"

"Thanks. Where've you been? I haven't seen you since the Human World."

Alan's smile dimmed. "Oh, 'ere and there. Too much to explain right now. I've come because Dorobonn sent me to fetch you."

Riley narrowed his eyes. "Where is he?"

"L'Za. Where the People of the Symbol lived. All three of you are to come. We will stay at Dorobonn's cabin for the night and then leave first thing at dawn."

Riley, Kelvin, and Joseph exchanged curious glances. "Alright. We'll go," Riley said. He was more exhausted than he wished to admit. He peered at the village, feeling a little more at peace. He still felt a bit restless with questions, but perhaps he could get some sleep tonight knowing that Zefa, at least, was safe.

After all, it wasn't as if the Dark Magic would last forever . . .

Epilogue

Caroline sat down and tried to focus on her surroundings. She peered closely at the bars of the cage which served as a makeshift prison for herself and Lunaira. Apparently, they were in some kind of cave. The walls were smooth and black—sparkling with a strange, ethereal light. No matter how often Caroline rubbed her eyes or blinked, everything was just out of focus. She had listened as that knight—Sir Leod, was it?—discussed with that magician Iradocc how they were going to hunt Riley down, along with another magician named Dorobonn. That name sounded familiar; she just couldn't place it. Wasn't he the one Riley had talked about who was teaching him magic? Caroline tucked her hair behind her ear. Riley had insisted he did not practice Dark Magic, and yet, with the way he'd been acting, Caroline had not believed him. Her heart wrenched at the memory of their argument.

Following hers and Lunaira's imprisonment, she had discovered from Iradocc that Riley didn't practice Dark Magic. Upon this realization, she could not help feeling guilty for pushing him away instead of listening to him. *But . . . he pushed* me *away.* That thought, nevertheless, didn't make her feel any better. She had allowed her emotions to cloud her better judgment. Growing up, her older siblings barely paid any attention to her and her parents were always busy. She did have younger siblings, but they were far younger than her and so she was often alone. She and Lunaira discussed how they would escape —if they could. Riley was still her friend. She wanted to tell him that but at the moment, all hope seemed lost. What if Riley did not survive his battle with Iradocc?

She knew quite well that Lunaira did not trust Riley. Lunaira had explained her own difficulties during childhood. Her mother had disappeared when Lunaira was quite young. A Dark Magician with a symbol had caused Lunaira's mother, the queen, to vanish without a trace. The Dark Magician had begged Lunaira's father for shelter from a terrible storm for the night. The king had scoffed, much to the Dark Magician's dismay, which then turned to rage. Consequently, the queen disappeared. Lunaira had not seen her mother in over seven years. Caroline did not know much about symbols, but she knew Riley, and he was *not* what Lunaira thought he was.

The sound of footsteps suddenly caught her attention and she saw Iradocc angrily walking by. "That boy's made a fool of me. I won't stand for it!"

Riley survived the battle! Caroline's heart flooded with a renewed sense of hope.

"Oh, Caroline. What will become of us?" Lunaira said.

"I don't know, but I'm sure we'll be alright." She placed her hand on Lunaira's, trying to reassure her friend, as well as herself. They were waiting for Iradocc to decide what he wanted to do with them. As she had listened to an earlier conversation, Caroline overheard that the . . . what was he called? A demolic? He wanted to use Caroline and Lunaira as bait in order to capture Riley. How? She did not know.

Iradocc slowed down as he passed by the cage a second time, and made eye contact with Caroline, but his gaze did not make her shiver as it had when she and Lunaira first arrived here. Was that remorse that she saw in his eyes? Iradocc quickly turned away before she could fully process it.

"When are you going to let us go?" Caroline asked, pensively.

"There will be no need to worry much longer. Your imprisonment will soon be over."

Caroline and Lunaira glanced at each other.

Iradocc's eyes shadowed mischievously.

Caroline's heart jumped into her throat. "What do you plan to do to us?" she remarked, trying to force as much anger in her voice as possible.

"You will see."

When Iradocc left, all was quiet again, until Lunaira asked, "Do you truly trust Riley, Caroline?"

"Yes. I do. It just doesn't make sense to me that he would practice Dark Magic. Heck, he battled Iradocc, who—from what we've now learned—*is* a Dark Magician! I don't know why Riley kept secrets from me, but he really is a good guy. And a true friend. I can only trust that he had his reasons."

Lunaira sighed. She did not seem convinced of Caroline's claim, but pressed the subject no further.

We will *get out of this. I know we will. Somehow, some way. Riley, where are you?*

The Star & Cicatrix Legacy Book Two

A Brother's Battle

Addison Dixon

Book #2 Blurb

The fate of the Human World and Ithara hang in the balance as Riley prepares to battle the Vile One. Unfortunately, Riley doesn't possess enough magic of his own to survive, much less win, requiring Dorobonn to transfer his own power to Riley. There is no other choice; only a human can turn back the magic from the Human World.

However, that leaves Dorobonn trapped in Arlock . . . and vulnerable to his brother Iradocc's resentment and hatred. When Dorobonn discovers a parchment that holds the secret to saving both worlds, Dorobonn must find a way to get it to Riley. But without his magic, Dorobonn entrusts the wrong person to deliver the message.

As he comes under attack, Riley is intent on saving the Human World with the help of his friends and a surprising ally. But the Dark Magic is strong, and the enemy will do anything to defeat Riley, including turning those closest to him against him. Only the power of love and forgiveness can banish the Dark Magic once and for all. But can Riley—and Dorobonn—find it in their hearts to forgive those who've betrayed them?

A Brother's Battle is the second book in The Star & Cicatrix Legacy series, a magical and enchanting fantasy about family, friendship, loyalty, and courage.

Acknowledgments

So many people were involved in the making of this book. First —I thank my parents for being there for me as I spent countless hours writing in notebooks (filling up 3 ½) with my story and then transitioning to my mom's old laptop. That version ended up being 600 pages! They pushed me to go after my dreams and follow my calling. Whatever it was, God wanted me to do. They expressed interest in my story before it was actually a book. The comics I drew—my parents would ask about the backgrounds and concepts of the characters. At eleven years old, I had no idea. Thanks, mom, for helping me with the first round of edits. She had a lot of patience. Sorry for running up to my room and reading when I was supposed to be doing schoolwork. I don't know how many times I did that, and I am thankful you continued to let me homeschool, following that spell.

Thank you, Papaw Crawford, for doing the second round of edits. I always enjoyed coming up to ya'll's house and looking over the revisions with you. You and Meemaw both also gave me endless encouragement, advice, and wisdom. So much of what Dorobonn tells Riley is based on what I have learned from ya'll and my parents. Basically, all of the older people in my life.

My family, in general, got me through the ups and downs of writing. G. Aunt Martha, I appreciate you editing the enormous book when it was initially printed. I'm glad to be exchanging letters with you again. College and other stuff can get super crazy! My siblings, cousins, aunts, uncles, grandparents . . . everyone has been there to help me. Friends, as well. Whether family-friends, or just my friends in general. The friends who have always been there for me. I won't mention any names for privacy's sake. Maybe you'll see some of yourselves in these characters *grins*. Chandler (though he's my brother, he's also my friend), wait'll you get to the sequel. Let's see if you can figure out which character(s) are based on you. Ha! Our little wrestling incident is practically documented in the second book. Many of the adventures in these books are loosely based on adventures my brother and I had together.

I also want to thank my beta readers for giving me honest feedback. It is valuable. I thank my editor, Sandra Byrd, for helping me so much through this writing journey. When I first sent you my manuscript, I actually feared what you'd think of it. Your words of confirmation and seeing potential in my work meant (and still means) a lot to me! Kate Heister and Serena Chase—thank ya'll too for your feedback.

Most of all—I thank my Heavenly Father for blessing me with stories to tell. Without Him, none of this would be possible.

Afterword

Throughout my life, I've always enjoyed telling stories. I drew little comics and pictures, imagining stories for the characters and scenarios I created. At eleven years old, I drew a rough sketch of Riley—at the time, I didn't have a name for him. I didn't typically name my characters at the time (too much work!). I vividly remember being at a friend's house the following year after spending the day at Six Flags Halloween Fright Fest. It'd influenced my imagination greatly.

While my friend decided to start writing for NaNoWriMo, I wanted to write for fun. As I was figuring out how to begin, I recalled the rough sketch of my character. I went through three names—I specifically remember. One of the names was Jonathan. The other . . . I think, was Peter. Neither seemed to match my character. The other one—Riley—was far more befitting. Finally, I remembered a guy named Riley from the movie *National Treasure.* He was fun-loving and sort of goofy. Seemed to fit my character a little more than the other two names.

That friend asked if I was continuing the book, and she was

surprised that I'd said yes. I was not known for sticking with projects. I wrote in the car, in restaurants, wherever I could. The adventures my younger brother, cousins, and I had heavily inspired many of Riley's adventures. The books I read, or that my mom read to my younger brother and me, also influenced my writing: Geronimo Stilton, Laurel the Woodfairy, the Boba Fett Star Wars series, Laura Ingalls, Anne of Green Gables, Eragon, and The Chronicles of Narnia. Funny enough, I didn't get into reading on my own until I was 11. Before that, I just let my mom read to me, or I read picture books (still do love reading those!) Traveling and video games inspired my imagination as well. I've always loved visiting historical sites. The mind needs history as a way of teaching it lessons and stories from the past.

I grew up imagining gnomes, elves, and fairies lived in my forest. I love trekking the paths and experiencing the magic in the air. That has never stopped. Once I typed down my first book (600 pages), my family recommended splitting it into three books. The book you're reading now is drastically different from the original, but the heart is still the same.

About the Author

Connect with Addison Dixon:

https://www.addisondixon.com/